LET ONE HUNDRED FLOWERS BLOOM

FENG JICAI

Let One Hundred Flowers Bloom

Translated by Christopher Smith

VIKING

VIKING

Published by the Penguin Group
Penguin Books Ltd, 27 Wrights Lane, London w8 5TZ, England
Penguin Books USA Inc., 375 Hudson Street, New York, New York 10014, USA
Penguin Books Australia Ltd, Ringwood, Victoria, Australia
Penguin Books Canada Ltd, 10 Alcorn Avenue, Toronto, Ontario, Canada M4V 3B2
Penguin Books (NZ) Ltd, 182–190 Wairau Road, Auckland 10, New Zealand

Penguin Books Ltd, Registered Offices: Harmondsworth, Middlesex, England

First published 1995
1 3 5 7 9 10 8 6 4 2
Text copyright © Feng Jicai, 1995
Translation copyright © Christopher Smith, 1995

Typeset by Datix International Limited, Bungay, Suffolk
Filmset in 13/15½ Monophoto Sabon

Made and printed in Great Britain by Clays Ltd, St Ives plc

A CIP catalogue record for this book is available from the British Library

ISBN 0-670-85805-6

Introduction

In June 1956, Chairman Mao, leader of the Communist Party in China, called upon the Chinese to 'Let one hundred flowers bloom, let one hundred schools of thought contend.' People responded eagerly to his invitation and criticisms and observations of the ruling Party flowed unreservedly and unsuspectingly. The Communist authorities reacted swiftly and ruthlessly. In the following year, Mao declared his anti-Rightist campaign against those people – 'Rightists' – who had in any way criticized the Party. Victims of the campaign were persecuted, imprisoned and exiled.

In 1966, after several years of relative calm, Mao felt his power threatened again, and announced the Great Proletarian Cultural Revolution: in order to build a new world, it was necessary to make a clean sweep of the traditional 'Four Olds', which comprised the philosophy, culture, customs and conventions of ancient times. Students and schoolchildren became members of the Red Guard, a militant youth movement, and threw themselves recklessly into carrying out Mao's instructions, even in the remotest parts of rural China.

We know today that the Cultural Revolution left in its wake millions of dead and vandalized a priceless cultural heritage. It finally ended with the death of Chairman Mao in 1976.

Prologue

The train had already gone through three stations. The other berths in the carriage had remained empty, thank goodness. Unless you're with a friend, you're better off alone on these long-distance journeys. I've always enjoyed my own company anyway, finding peace and tranquillity in solitude.

Night had fallen several hours ago. All of a sudden a dazzling shaft of light shot in from outside the carriage. Before I could decide whether it was a train coming in the opposite direction or whether we were pulling into a station, the train shuddered to a halt. Half the water in my mug slopped to the floor. A child had been startled awake in one of the other compartments and was wailing. I pressed my face against the icy window and looked outside. We had arrived at the station for Guo Jia Dian, a village situated on the plains of the Liao River. Not a soul stirred between the slogan-covered stone pillars of the station building. The freezing winter wind had torn down the big character posters* and had rolled them into balls which were now skittering across the platform. After the briefest of stops, the train's steam

* Asterisks signal words which can be found in the Glossary, page 105.

3

whistle screeched and I heard the sound of doors being slammed shut. These noises were followed by another judder which announced our departure. It seemed as if I was still going to have the compartment all to myself. I lay down, turned off the overhead light and switched on the little wall lamp by my pillow instead. Beneath the dim electric glow, I let my thoughts and imagination wander, luxuriating in the peace and quiet which is only possible when one is alone. Then I heard the sound of a door being pulled open. Damn! Someone was coming.

I sat up hurriedly and switched on the main light. I couldn't see anyone, but an unwieldy cardboard box was being shoved into the compartment. After the box came to rest, a man appeared. Just as I'd made up my mind to say hello, he panted heavily, took off his chilly cotton padded overcoat and threw it on to the bunk. He then turned round and kicked a scruffy sports bag into the compartment. The bag's zip was broken and the bag itself had been fastened in the middle with a piece of string. He was also carrying a wooden portfolio case which was covered in grimy green cloth a little frayed about the edges. As soon as he'd got his things inside, he turned round and closed the compartment door. His movements were as jumpy as those of a person travelling without a ticket. Since entering the compartment he had ig-nored me completely, and was now looking around for somewhere to put his cardboard box. When he sat down, I asked, 'Is it cold out?' Acting as though he hadn't heard me, he got up and started looking around again, eventually deciding to push the box into a space above the door. He seemed to be having some difficulty lifting the box, but just as I'd decided to ask him whether he needed a hand, he grunted with effort, his bottom directly in front of my face. I'd never met such an ignorant and rude person! Nor did he bother to apologize once the box was safely stowed; he just sat there staring with eyes that were as lifeless as those of a dead fish. Then he squinted at me as though I were a real strain on his eyes. I got the feeling that this was just the start of what promised to be a very unpleasant journey.

Deciding to ignore him, I leant my head against the side of the carriage and pretended to nod off. However, after a while the man started to get restless: first he struck a match and started to smoke, his exhalations sounding as though he was blowing out the smoke; then he started muttering to himself, saying things like 'This train's going too slowly . . .', 'Let's warm our hands . . .', and 'It's so dark, it's so so dark . . .'. It occurred to me that he was probably a bit crazy. He started to twist and shuffle on his seat. One minute he'd be sitting down and the next he'd be standing up. He kept adjusting the position of his cardboard box. I opened my eyes a crack and surreptitiously watched him. He was standing on tiptoe and covering the box with his padded cotton jacket. After this, instead of sitting down, he opened the jacket so that a corner of the box was sticking out. I noticed with curiosity that the corner was torn open. What could it be that needed to be kept warm but also needed fresh air? It had to be an animal of some kind. My first thought was that he was secretly

5

transporting a chicken or a cat or a dog . . . but then why hadn't it crowed or meowed or barked? Even if it was a rabbit it should have made some kind of noise moving about. Then something even stranger happened. The man turned round to look at me and, thinking I was asleep, gently climbed on top of the bunk. He put his mouth to the hole and whispered, 'You must be suffocating! Never mind, we'll be there in the morning!'

My God! A slave trader! On reflection, I realized that you'd never fit a grown-up into a metre-long box . . . it must be a child. But then what was he doing carrying that portfolio case? Maybe pretending to be an artist was his cover.

I waited until he sat down again and scrutinized him more closely. Luckily, I was sitting in the shadow: with my eyes almost closed like that he wouldn't be able to tell whether I was awake or asleep. The man's hair was as messy as a haystack in autumn and his flat-featured face was covered in dirt, as though he'd just crawled out of a hole. His scrawny hands were a mass of scars, doubtless the result of some fight. As I looked at him again, I noticed that the top buttons of his clothes were all undone, from his old army uniform and tatty sweat-shirt right down to the shirt with a torn collar that he was wearing underneath. At first glance his sorry appearance made him look like an escaped convict. However, closer scrutiny revealed that his clothes were splashed all over with paint, newer stains piled on top of the older ones. He had a kind of undisci-plined, careless and even rather exceptional air about him, though it was difficult to say whether it was his face or just his general demeanour which gave this impression. A dejected and destitute artist perhaps? But then how could he afford to travel soft sleeper class?* And how did all this fit in with the mysterious cardboard box? I couldn't figure it out. Curiosity and a general feeling of unease eventually made me blurt out, 'What's in the box?'

He almost leapt out of his seat. 'You frightened me! I thought you were asleep.' The colour had drained from his face – there was obviously something unusual in that box.

He stared at me and then replied, 'Let me ask you something, and then we'll talk.'

What! Him ask me a question? Before I could open my mouth, he launched right in. 'You're an author, aren't you? I'm right, aren't I?'

'What, me?' I didn't know what to say. In those days it wasn't at all clear whether being an author was glorious or shameful. I laughed bitterly. 'I have written things in the past.'

'I knew it! I recognized you the minute I set eyes on you.' He relaxed visibly, his alarmed expression rippling away in an instant. He leant back. 'You wouldn't know me. I'm one of your readers. I often used to see your photo in the papers. I even read the articles denouncing you . . . which I found very upsetting, needless to say.'

These few words served to break the ice. I began to think that my previous suspicions were groundless.

'You . . .' There were some questions I wanted to

ask him, but he fished out a crumpled packet of cigarettes from his pocket and then plucked out an old dog-end that he hadn't been able to bring himself to throw away. He lit the cigarette, dragged on it twice viciously, then blew out the smoke as before. Separated from me by a thick pall of smoke, he announced: 'Let me tell you a story!' Seeing my astonished look, he pointed upwards and added, 'Didn't you want to hear about the box ... and about me? Well, it's all in the story. I've never told this story to anyone else, but I want to tell it to you ...'

Something in his eyes told me that he trusted me. Enjoying the public's trust is the greatest tribute a writer can receive. As a famous author you often get complete strangers coming up to you and telling you things which they have always kept locked away in their hearts. It's as though they believe that you alone will care about and understand what they have to say; you end up gaining much more than their secret.

He turned his head and stared at the black icy landscape outside the window with those smoky eyes of his. After a moment's contemplation, he turned back. It was as though he'd swapped his old eyes for a new set: these were shining, piercing, threatening, as though some irrepressible force was going to explode from them. He put out his cigarette, using his thumb and forefinger. 'It's like this ...' he began. Even during the tumultuous upheavals of the past few years I had never heard a story monstrous enough to make me lose my composure ... But who could have guessed that such a devastating story existed?

He agreed to let me write it. For his protection I've always kept it hidden away in the recesses of my memory. It is only now that I have been able to commit it to paper.

Chapter 1

I'll begin at the start of the 1960s when I'd just graduated from the Beijing Academy of Fine Arts after studying oil painting. I can say without boasting that I was acknowledged to be the best of my year. I was convinced that I would end up working in a specialist department like the Art Gallery, the Fine Arts Press or the Fine Arts Research Institute. Those departments were keen to have me too. A girl from my year I really liked found out that there was a good chance that the Academy of Fine Arts would keep me on as an assistant. I was so keen in those days and desperate to make my mark on society. 'March into life and the future wielding your brush', I used to repeat to myself all day long, grinning from ear to ear. So when I finally got the notification telling me the department to which I had been assigned, I was flabbergasted. The Number Two Porcelain Factory, Qianxi County: a place so obscure we hadn't even joked about being sent there. At first I thought there had been a mistake. When I looked and saw my name – Hua Xiayu – there on the notice board as plain as day, the paper was black before my eyes. Everything I had looked forward to was obliterated by the black paper: all my aspirations, ambitions and plans. Even my girlfriend. As I stood at Beijing railway station waiting for the Qianxi train, it still felt as if I was in a dream. I couldn't believe this was happening. Why? How? What had gone wrong?

At the time, I suspected that my assignment to this job was the work of the head of department. The two of us held diametrically-opposed views on art: in a nutshell, he regarded art as an academic discipline and I regarded it as a living thing. The two of us often reached deadlock on the subject but the majority of students agreed with me. I had badly wounded his self-esteem . . . there was no way he would have kept me on. In fact, I was doing him a great injustice: my misfortune had nothing to do with him. No one could guess what really happened . . . anyway, I'll get back to all of this later.

Fate really started putting the boot in. First, I was banished to this dump; then there was no one there to meet me when I arrived. I had to shoulder my bags and start walking. The further I walked, the angrier I became; I nearly turned back on several occasions.

However, when I eventually found myself standing outside the gates of the porcelain factory looking in, to my surprise everything changed. The sight that greeted my eyes left me stunned. I threw my bags on the ground. The huge courtyard was covered with countless pieces of pottery waiting to be fired in the kilns: bowls, huge vats, bottles, jars and pots vied with each other for space. The unfired items had an untamed look about them. They possessed a natural and elemental beauty in their rough, unfinished, purple and white state. All the kiln workers were naked from the waist up, their tough, supple backs burned black by the sun and shining with sweat. The big furnace in the background looked as though it had been painted all over in brick red and golden brown. It was the purest and most glorious blaze of colour I had ever seen. Real-life colours are always so full of vitality, so fresh. I immediately fell in love with the place. I rushed through the gate to report my arrival.

The factory's Party Secretary was called Luo Tieniu. He looked like a little pedlar. His body was short and twisted like a squashed shoe-box. He treated me with deference, courteous but as though he were hiding something. He showed me around the kiln and the paint-room. The workers mostly ignored me, the younger ones glancing curiously then quickly getting their heads back down to work, and the older ones not even bothering to look up. It occurred to me that people from rural backwaters probably dreaded university graduates from the cities. Nevertheless, I gave them a benevolent and cordial little smile.

If you have never worked in ceramics, you couldn't possibly imagine what an intriguing world it is. Every bottle and jar and even the most ordinary china bowl has to go through dozens of processes before it is finished. Each of these painstaking and mysterious processes is carried out in its own particular way. Every month, the young girls working at the moulds would pour thirteen thousand *jin** of porcelain clay into the moulds. Under the workshops were the huge cooking ranges that made the rooms feel like the inside of steaming baskets, but whose purpose was to dry out the clay quickly. In midsummer the heat would get so unbearable that even the unmarried girls would strip to the waist without embarrassment.

In the workshop I noticed a tall and robust old man making a vase. He put a lump of soft clay on the potter's wheel and worked the pedals with his feet. He raised his hands and, without his fingers seeming to move, created a vase that was at once simple but full of life. His style of pottery did not emulate the neatness and meticulous detail of the Jingdezhen* school. At first glance it appeared clumsy, but it actually possessed a kind of simplicity and power. This was especially noticeable in the vases he produced, each one of which breathed so much life and vitality that one could almost imagine it talking out loud. Moved by his skill, I asked him, 'Master, how do you do that?'

My genuine admiration did not seem to please him, however. Turning to look at me, he replied harshly, 'I use my hands.' This irritating answer landed like a lump of clay in the pit of my stomach. I decided to ignore him from then on. Actually, I've never been able to hate anyone and I soon forgot all about it.

Secretary Luo called over a tall young man. His skin was as smooth as silk and he had a broad grin on his face as he was introduced to me. His name was Luo Jiaju and he was the head of the painting section which I was about to join. I was very pleased about this as he was the first friendly person I had met so far. Insisting on carrying my bags for me, he took me to the rear courtyard to see the dormitory. He said that he had known for a long time that I would be coming and had been looking forward to it. When he said that he hoped I would be his teacher, he sounded completely sincere; when I was at the Fine Arts Academy, amateur painters had often displayed a similar kind of ardent respect. I found out later that Luo Jiaju enjoyed a very unusual position in the factory: not only was he Secretary Luo's nephew, he was also a distinguished scholar. Extremely intelligent, he had joined the factory when he was nineteen. His knowledge of colours and glazes was even more extensive than an old woman's knowledge of cookery. He could sketch, paint in the traditional Chinese style or in watercolours; he could do calligraphy in both cursive and official styles and was completely self-taught.

He pointed towards a dingy room and said, 'Don't be angry. All the people in the factory are locals, so there isn't a proper dormitory here. A few years ago a relative of one of the factory's accountants came here from Qinhuangdao looking for work . . . he was an artist too. There was nowhere else for him to go, so this is where he stayed. It used to be two rooms. Since he left it's just been used for storing rubbish. When I heard you were coming, I managed to get the outer room cleared. When there's more space we'll get the inner room cleared too . . .'

I took a good look at the room; it really wasn't fit for human habitation. It was only three or four metres square. Even if you could ignore the size, it still looked as if it was made of unfired clay. The floor was yellow earth. The whitewash on the walls had more or less all been rubbed off. The ceiling wasn't papered over and you could see the mortar and the dirty bark-covered rafters. There was no door connecting the inner and outer rooms, just wooden planks. An acrid smell seeped through the gaps between the planks. There were only a few very basic pieces of furniture and the windowsill was carpeted with a layer of grass roots. What, you think that made me angry? Not at all; I'm not in the least bit concerned about that kind of thing. Given the choice between a palace and a forest, I would probably choose the forest. I get all the inspiration for my art from nature. Take the back window in my room, for example. The view out on to the wide expanse of river bank and silent wilderness melted into the undecorated state of the inside of my room with a kind of unschooled and natural beauty. It was fantastic.

I was only in my twenties. I had left the Fine Arts Academy behind me, but not art. Everything I saw around me thrilled my artistic sensibilities. Every object, living or lifeless, seemed to be shining, breathing, resonating. Even the sun's rays, the wind, the undulating shade of the trees, the silent, microscopic, sparkling specks of dust had feelings. And do you know, night-time colours are richer and more vibrant than those of the day? I felt as though all my nerve-endings were on the surface of my skin; my sensitivity often left me in a state of nervous excitement. I liked the people at the factory not only because when they worked it looked like a scene from a painting, but also because their simple and honest natures made their faces very interesting to draw. My urge to paint them was often irresistible.

However, I gradually realized that my feelings towards them were not reciprocated. Except for Luo Jiaju, hardly anyone ever spoke to me. Although people from the countryside normally love having their portraits done, none of them would let me paint them. Why were they all shunning me?

Early one morning I was leaning over the tap and brushing my teeth when the factory's driver, Cui Dajiao, suddenly grabbed me by the shoulder. He bellowed in my ear, 'Are you a counter-revolutionary?'

His question left me dazed for a moment. By the time I'd picked up a glass of water and rinsed the toothpaste from my mouth, I saw his broad-shouldered figure disappearing in the distance.

Although it was true that Cui Dajiao was a little dense, he hadn't sounded as if he was just thoughtlessly shooting his mouth off. In spite of myself I started after him to find out what he meant. He glowered at me, his very posture making it clear that he regarded me as a criminal of the most despicable kind. 'Don't play the innocent. Everyone in the factory knows. You've come here to reform yourself!'

When I heard these words I immediately thought of my black registration document, Secretary Luo's false courtesy and all those faces in the factory that had refused to look me in the eye. So this was what was behind it all. I had never done anything wrong, but after 1957 informing upon others was rife. Had I ever privately said anything bad in front of someone else? Who can remember everything one's ever said? In any case, I could feel that there was 'something' out there in the dark, stalking me, pressing in on me and threatening me. I began to suffer from frequent anxiety attacks.

In the wake of all this, my attitude to those around me naturally changed. If someone was cold to me I put it down to the stigma of that 'something'. I shunned contact with others, feeling as awkward as if I really had done something wrong. The artistic sensitivity that I had felt for everything around me gradually diminished. Life seemed to become colourless. I worked during the daylight hours and then retired alone to my room. I didn't feel like doing anything, and my paintbrush dried out so much it became like an awl. Occasionally I told myself that I couldn't simply stop painting, but when I did try to paint the results were spiritless, gutless and lifeless; after I'd finished I didn't want to see them again.

During that period my one and only diversion and comfort was that back window. I propped my pillow high with books so that I could look directly out of the window. Every window frame in the world is like a picture frame filled with living things. My picture frame was filled with a gloomy and ancient river with a sluggish current. I could see right up to the point where it merged into the horizon. The river was so shallow that there were never any boats on it;

not on the stretches near by nor further off in the distance. The river's banks consisted of great mud flats, dried into a hard crust by the sun and then cracked into a series of deep trenches. The only remotely impressive things were the jagged fissured rocks which lay exposed in several places. The grass seemed to be congenitally stunted and yellowed and withered before it was ever green. The river's banks stretched out into the distance, gradually softening and dissipating like smoke to form a cold, boundless, alkaline wilderness. One side of this wilderness was often shrouded in fog and even on a clear day you could not see its boundaries; the other side ended with a dense belt of trees about twenty *li** in the distance. This belt of trees was like a mystical barrier. When the birds took off from it they shed a brilliant sheet of crystalline sunlight that made everything on the ground sit up and take notice. When they flew over they brought sound, life and a feeling of unrestrained freedom to the vast and lonely landscape in the window frame. They brought a feeling of contentment and comfort. When they flew away from the trees and far into the distance they took my heart with them too.

Chapter 2

About a month after I had arrived there was a day's public holiday and I slept in late. When I eventually pushed open the door of my room a most peculiar sight greeted my eyes. A black dog was sitting outside the doorway. I couldn't see his face too clearly as he was black all over, but he gave the impression of being both strong and rather ferocious. He had a pair of large drooping ears. A soft and slobbery pink tongue lolled out of his half-open mouth and quivered in time to his panting breath. I knew that only ferocious dogs pant this way. The dog didn't whine or bark. He was like a dignified palace guard, stern and seasoned. He squatted there and didn't move, valiantly puffing out a chest that was covered in long, downy fur. I wanted to fetch some hot water, and tried several times to cross the threshold with my thermos flask; but each time I was forced to retreat in the face of that stern gaze. I carried on trying for about ten minutes but he showed no inclination to move. I decided to try and circle round him. My experience of dogs when I had been a child growing up in the countryside was that the more you ignore them, the less they try to frighten you. This dog, however, had obviously come to see me personally. He remained quite still as I walked through the doorway, but as I tried to walk past him he got up, moved nonchalantly to a spot two paces in front of me and sat down again. When I tried to go round the other side, he simply repeated his manoeuvre. He wasn't going to let me past for love nor money. I was trapped. I stood there at a loss, staring at the dog and grasping my empty thermos flask. What did he want? Suddenly, I heard a merry laugh from up ahead. The odious Cui Dajiao was standing there, leaning against the brick wall of the workshop, and having a good laugh at my expense. Infuriated, I put down the thermos and shouted at the dog: 'What are you staring at? I'll thrash you!' I turned round and grabbed the broom that was standing by the door. At this point a husky voice yelled, 'Don't move!'

It was Luo Changgui, the old man at the potter's wheel who had humiliated me on my first day at the factory. He walked over and shouted, 'Go away, Jet!'

The dog stepped back a pace. I invited Luo Chang-gui into the room. As it was the old man's first visit, I wanted to brew him some tea, but . . . awkwardly, I pointed to the empty thermos and then to the dog who was still standing guard outside the door. Luo Changgui laughed. 'You don't want to be frightened of him. He's a stray. He doesn't come here often and he'll probably go away on his own in a minute.'

'He doesn't look like a stray,' I replied.

'You must have good eyesight,' said Luo Changgui. 'How can you tell?'

'Just an impression.' These three words were never far from the lips of the students at the Fine Arts Academy.

Luo Changgui frowned.

'What is it?'

'Nothing. Actually, you're right: he is tame. He used to belong to an oil-presser on Number Two Street. His coat was really glossy back then because his master used to brush it with oil. But food was pretty scarce a couple of years ago and the dog ate too much. His master didn't have enough to feed him, so he gave him away to a timber mill. When he got home again after taking him to the mill, his master discovered that somehow the dog had managed to get back before him. He steeled himself again and took him to a brick factory outside town. Because he was worried that he might escape again, his master tied him to a post with a chain. That night it rained all night. But, sure enough, the dog reappeared, sopping wet and with half the chain still hanging from his neck. The back of his neck was covered in blood where he had strained at the chain until it snapped. This time when he got back he immediately dived under the bed. He refused to come out when they called him and he wouldn't eat the food they gave him. It was as if he knew the reason that he had been sent away in the first place. He kept refusing food until he was half dead from starvation, and even then he only ate a little. After that, when he got really hungry he would go scavenging outside rather than steal food from the house. Clever, eh?'

'So how did he become a stray?' This dog's story was like a powerful magnet drawing me towards him.

'It happened last year. The oil-presser's family moved away to Tangshan. As you're not allowed to keep dogs in the big cities, the oil-presser fed him alcohol to get him drunk and then left him behind. When he woke up, his family was gone and he was a stray. He used to roam about all day and steal food from people's houses. He often used to come to our factory as there are always left-over bones and vegetables round the back of the canteen. To start with, Cui Dajiao used to chase him away, but then he managed to catch a thief who had stolen some bottles. As he had managed to make himself useful, Cui Dajiao didn't chase him off after that. Now he comes and goes as he pleases.'

'How come no one keeps him as a pet?'

'Originally Secretary Luo wanted to but the dog wasn't interested. Maybe the oil-presser treated him too badly and he doesn't trust humans!' Luo Changgui gave a significant laugh. Old people's laughs always seem to imply some other meaning. 'Anyway, once a tame dog turns stray it's very difficult to change it back again. He's a good dog, though . . .'

'What did you say his name was?'

'Jet. That's the name that the oil-presser gave him,' replied Luo Changgui.

I shot a glance at Jet, that extraordinary ill-fated dog. My feelings towards him had completely changed. His shaggy canine exterior concealed many characteristics that would draw gasps of admiration if seen in a human. His experience had been that of a human being, not a dog.

Then Luo Changgui spoke to me: 'Don't take any notice of him. I've come round to see your paintings; I've heard they're not bad.'

When I heard his reason for coming I felt a mixture of unease and overwhelming gratitude.

It's very difficult for an outsider to imagine the secrecy of the porcelain business. In order to preserve the factory's trade secrets, nearly all of the hundred or more people employed there were from the Luo clan. People from other families found it very difficult to stay on. Unless they were like the despicable Cui Dajiao and not involved in the production of the pottery, they would always get elbowed out. The only two people of any importance in the factory were Luo Changgui and Luo Jiaju. I wasn't at all interested in the fine type of vase produced by Luo Jiaju but I was captivated by the vases and colourful glazes of Luo Changgui. I was particularly fascinated by the glazes. They were one colour when they were painted on and another after they had been fired. They seemed to go through some kind of unfathomable alchemic process, and all kinds of nuances, suggestions and feelings that weren't originally present could suddenly appear. Say, for example, you painted a fish and a few strands of duckweed. If the heat of the furnace was too high the fish might be transformed into the reflection of a boat and the duckweed might metamorphose into a dense storm of snowflakes. It was a new world to me, a world that was more mysterious than any ancient painting I had ever seen.

I had expressed a wish to learn art from Luo Changgui instead of being cooped up in the paintshop every day, painting blue rims on to bowls. I had been slightly nervous that Luo Jiaju might be displeased, but to my surprise he had smilingly agreed. On my first day in Luo Changgui's workshop, Luo Changgui had tested me. He asked me to carry a freshly drawn metre-high vase over to the other side of the workshop. To show my enthusiasm I grabbed hold of the vase with all my strength. Thud! The vase crumpled in on itself like a giant eggshell and spread out all over the table. I lost my balance and landed on top of it. Covered from head to toe in clay, I heard the workshop erupt with laughter. The old man gathered the clay from the table without saying a word. In the twinkling of an eye he had made another vase, identical in size and shape to the one I had destroyed. Afterwards, he placed a hand on either side and miraculously picked it up, despite the fact that it weighed several tens of *jin*. He carried it a couple of steps and then put it down next to me. Then he went off again without saying a single word, leaving me to stand next to it like a dunce.

I was therefore extremely nervous of this old man. Fearing that he might have no appreciation of oil paintings and that this might make him despise me still further, I started by digging out the copies that I had made of classical Song and Yuan landscapes. I had painted these as part of the Fine Arts Academy's traditional art course, together with flower and bird

paintings. To my surprise, he was a lot more interested in the oil paintings with their abstract shapes
and stronger colours. He started off by staring at
them as though he were trying to decipher them.
Gradually his face relaxed and all of a sudden he
clapped the canvas twice. This was just like the
double clap he always gave himself when he had
made a particularly nice vase and was feeling pleased
with himself.

Then I noticed that the dog had disappeared from
the doorway. When I looked again I saw that he was
actually still there. His body was hidden behind the
wall and you could only see part of his face as he
stared timidly into the room. He looked just like a
child! The sight of him aroused in me a mixture of
pity, sympathy and warmth. As he wouldn't come in
when I called him, I wanted to go and give him a
hug.

Luo Changgui grabbed my arm: 'He roams around
outside all day; he's filthy.' Then he frowned and
said, 'It's odd, he normally doesn't like to come near
people. The smell of oil paints in this room must be
like the smell at the oil-presser's . . .'

It was very odd. From that day on, Jet used to
come round a lot. I couldn't say for certain why he
came to see me. He even seemed to be able to
remember dates: he always came round on my days
off! I would be doing something or other in my room
and then when I looked up I would see his head
poking round the door. He obviously wanted to
make friends with me, but no matter how much I
called to him he wouldn't come in the room. I even

26

tried to entice him in with food, but the harder I tried the more reluctant he was to come in. The only part of him that would enter was his blue shadow, cast by the sun's rays. We still hadn't established bonds of trust. As the saying goes: those who have suffered misfortune find it hard to trust; apparently it's the same with dogs.

I had an idea. When he came round I nodded at him as I would do to an old friend, then picked up my easel and started to paint. To avoid arousing his suspicions, I paid him no further attention. Once I painted continuously for an hour without looking up. I was sure he was in the doorway, so I carried on painting. Two and a half hours had passed in all when, out of the corner of my eye, I saw a fluffy shadow creeping towards me. My heart started to pound and I was scared that the brush would slip from my hand and frighten him off. I felt something furry and heavy pressing against my leg. We were actually next to each other. I bottled up my excitement and carried on painting, painting, painting until all the sunlight had gone from the room. I was exhausted. I'd never found it so tiring before. I looked down and saw him leaning against my leg, dreaming sweet dreams ... at least that's what I imagined.

From then on I had a companion.

He was definitely not a home dog. He didn't like spending all his time in my room. Sometimes he would disappear for ten days or more and I would never know where he was or what he was doing. When he really missed me he would reappear. As soon as he arrived he would nudge my leg with his head, bite the leg of my trousers and lick my hand. He would play around during the day and then sleep at my feet at night. If there was any noise outside he would go and see what was going on, all alert, or he would simply stay on guard all night outside the door. He was extremely clever and would learn anything you taught him. He understood almost immediately when I taught him how to open the door. He learnt to lean on the door handle so that he could come and go whenever he liked. When I said, 'Raise your left paw', he would give me his left paw; when I said, 'Raise your right paw', he gave me his right paw. He never begged for food but of course I would buy some for him every time the canteen sold spare ribs, braised trotters or offal cooked in soy sauce. He definitely didn't come round for the food. I used to stroke his head and ask, 'Why do you always come round to see me?'

He would stare back at me without making a sound. He seemed to be saying that I should know why.

Chapter 3

As it turned out, I was destined to have an even closer companion. As soon as she arrived on the scene, Jet was relegated to the background. Her name was Luo Junjun.

It was dusk. Luo Jiaju produced the girl out of thin air. He said that she was an art teacher from the county town's Number One Secondary School and she wanted to meet me because she admired my work.

My first impression of her was of a sort of hazy warmth. I noted her long and slender legs, her chin, her softly rounded shape. The thing which I found most refreshing and unique, however, was the fact that there was not a sharp line in her whole body. Her outline was hazy, as though she was inseparable from the background. Whichever background she stood before seemed temporarily to take on her colour, her light and even her ambience to form a beautiful picture.

Thinking back to that first day, I remember how I fumbled to get my pictures out for her and how I talked and talked. I can't remember a single thing I said. I remember feeling as though my mouth was too small to voice all my ideas and so they were left buzzing around my head like bees inside a hive. She hardly said a word. Light flashed from her long-lashed eyes, like the pure reflected light which shines from a mountain stream when the snow has melted in springtime. After she left I used vermilion, ochre, an earthy yellow and a vibrant green to mix together a warm colour which I then painted all over the dark walls. That colour was her. It was as though she was melted all over the wall. I spent the whole night in a state of nervous excitement, staring at that colour.

That first day, although Luo Jiaju was sitting in the room too, I completely forgot he was there. After that, Luo Junjun didn't ask him along. She used to come on her own, bringing paintings for me to look at. I heard that she had grown up in Qingdao and that her father had abandoned her and her mother. After her mother died she had no relatives left in Qingdao, so she came here to live with her aunt. She had studied for two years at the Qingdao Academy of Arts and Crafts but there was certainly nothing special about her paintings. In fact, she lacked even the most basic technique; her paintings were like the wild scrawls of a little girl. However, her feel for art was strong. When she explained the ideas which lay behind those naïve pictures, it was brilliant! She really was very artistic. The people I dislike talking to most are the ones who are quite skilled but who have no appreciation of art. You can talk to them until the cows come home and they'll still stare at you blankly. With Luo Junjun, on the other hand, you could just say what you felt and, no matter how subtle or abstract the idea might be, she would understand it completely. Later I realized that she was like a lot of other girls, bursting with imagination and full of enthusiasm for poetry and literature. She particularly loved Turgenev's novels, sometimes comparing herself with Lida and sometimes with Assia. Does it seem laughable that she should walk through the busy streets of this county town thinking such thoughts? All her qualities had been formed in idyllic Qingdao, with its seagulls and country villas, in the household of her engineer father . . . And I had met a girl like her in a cut-off little backwater. It was miraculous!

I decided that it was fate that had brought her here and brought me here, fate that had made the two of us meet.

When I corrected her paintings with her, she would bring over a short wooden bench and sit next to me. Her gaze would gradually turn from her paintings to my face. Those long-lashed eyes would stare at me as though dazed, displaying surprise, admiration, excitement and confusion. Very soon – after she had come to see me five or six times and we knew each other better – she would sing songs, recite poetry and dance for me. I would sit and watch her as she gambolled about, singing and dancing with childlike innocence and pleasure. My heart felt like a wilderness that had turned green at the first touch of spring. She used to keep herself amused by creating the atmosphere of a novel all around her; and she wanted to include me in it too, so that we could enjoy it together. She used to like leaning against my shoulder and murmuring to herself, putting her artistic visions into words. She had a flower-patterned blouse that she loved to wear. She would slip into my room while I was out and would stand in a dimly lit part of the room so that when I got back my first sight of her would be like finding a painting. She made me rediscover life's charms. The world was suddenly ablaze with colour. Every conceivable object distilled into an essence of colour, bubbling and flowing across my palette. My brushes began to overheat! I would leap out of bed in the middle of the night, looking for my easel in a blind painting frenzy. But it all came upon me too violently. I lacked the cool-headedness necessary for art. When I picked up the brush I had no idea what I wanted to draw. One evening she stayed really late. It was raining outside and I said, 'I'll walk you back.'

She looked me right in the eye: 'You're throwing me out?' Her gaze scalded me and I looked quickly away. The best artist in the world couldn't have done justice to her eyes: they were smouldering.

'Why don't you look at me?' She spoke very softly but with a rich tremor in her voice. It was as though she was scared of something, but she clearly intended to overcome her timidity.

'It's too late, I'm worried people will talk about you . . .'

Suddenly she grabbed my wrist, tugged open the door and, against my better judgement, dragged me outside into the courtyard. Through the sound of the pouring rain she yelled, 'Let them stare. We'll do whatever we please!'

We were so much in love, and desperate to get married. No one objected openly, but getting it sorted out ended up being very awkward. If it wasn't having trouble finding the right person to prepare the necessary papers, it was discovering that the crucial seal was locked away in a cupboard and couldn't be retrieved. Then Luo Junjun disappeared for three days. The first day she failed to appear I waited; the second day I started to get worried; the third day I decided to go and find her. Things had moved so fast between us that I hadn't even met her aunt and uncle. I learnt that this uncle of hers sold stationery at the county supply and marketing co-operative and also that he was very grumpy. Had she run into difficulties? Maybe she was too young to get married . . .

She came back that evening. Although she was still chatting away and laughing, she didn't mention the marriage formalities and I got the impression that her laughter was a little forced. Her eyes were also a bit red. I asked her what had happened and a cloud of worry passed over her beautiful face: 'Tell me something. Have you ever made any political mistakes?'

'No, absolutely not! What's the matter?' Thinking that this answer alone wouldn't be enough to get rid of the frown between her eyebrows, I added, 'Don't you believe me?'

She rested her head against my shoulder. 'Forgive me, I shouldn't have asked you. I believe you're a good person and I'll never leave you.'

I was astonished. What did she have to say that for?

I'm so stupid. I have no trouble joining separate

abstract artistic concepts, but I simply didn't make the connection between what she'd just said and Cui Dajiao's accusing questions when I'd first arrived.

Then ten days passed with no sign of her. Each one of those days felt as though it was at least eighty hours long and each new day felt longer than the one before. I began to suspect that I'd been dumped. The world felt empty.

On the eleventh day, however, I heard her voice outside the window. I saw her standing on that expanse of wilderness framed by the window and she was waving at me. Her bright yellow dress was dazzling in the sunlight. As I went over she beckoned to me to hurry up and look at something. Spread out on the green turf was a square of freshly picked yellow chrysanthemums. Each side of the square was nearly a metre long. She gesticulated that I should pick up the flowers, the expression on her face both happy and mysterious. I gently picked the golden petals and found a sheet of paper underneath. It was a marriage licence! I lifted up the sealed licence – as beautiful as it was hard to come by – and fell to my knees on the grass. I was delirious! She lay down on the grass and said to me: 'If I die, bury me like this. This wildflower is the same colour as me . . . you must lay it on my grave . . .'

I covered her mouth with my hands.

Pushing my hands away, she continued earnestly: 'That's not all. After you've finished burying me you must commit suicide!' After she said this she inexplicably burst into tears and wouldn't stop despite all my pleas. Later, laughing at herself, she snatched the licence from my hands and started singing and gam-bolling round me like a lamb. She shouted out, 'We've won!', but teardrops were glistening on her long eyelashes like tiny pearls of dew on blades of grass. 'We've won. Why aren't you celebrating?'

I nodded my head and smiled, but I wasn't sure over whom we had triumphed.

Almost every single person in the county town seemed to have heard about our marriage. I only then found out that Junjun had had a huge argument with her family before getting the marriage licence. She had deeply wounded her aunt's feelings. Her aunt hadn't any children of her own and she treated Junjun as her little girl. Junjun had given up every-thing and my love for her increased accordingly. I heard that the reason that her uncle had opposed the marriage had something to do with Luo Jiaju. But why? It was true that things had been a little tense between Luo Jiaju and me when I had been working in the paintshop, but since I had moved to Luo Changgui's team, the two of us hadn't had any run-ins at all. I suddenly remembered that the first time I had met Junjun, it was Luo Jiaju who had brought her along. Maybe the two of them . . . I gradually sensed what was behind it all.

I pulled the blanket over our heads and said: 'There's only the two of us here. The tables and chairs won't hear anything. Tell me the truth . . . Is Luo Jiaju in love with you?'

She didn't make a sound; I was just aware of that special fragrance that her body gave off. She didn't deny it.

I carried on: 'Were you in love with him? It's even more important you tell me the truth about that.' She was silent for a moment and when she spoke she didn't answer me. 'I only love you. You alone, now and for ever!' She said it really urgently. Before I had a chance to say anything, she gave me a ferocious hug and pressed her lips tight against mine for what seemed an age.

This was the hidden reason, I now realized, for the deterioration in my relationship with Luo Jiaju. But Luo Jiaju's face was still always wreathed in smiles. In fact, he grinned so hard that you could barely see his eyes and it became even harder to know what he was really thinking. When he bumped into me he would even banter: 'When you get married, I'll be there, teasing the newly-weds!' Could he really be that generous-spirited?

I decided to pull out all the stops to make sure that the happiest day of my life went off perfectly. I asked Luo Changgui for permission to fire some plates in a style of my own choosing. Luo Changgui very generously agreed. This really was a big favour as the factory's ceramics had previously only been made according to strict rules. I drew upon my own observations – gathered over a long period of time – about the qualities, properties and effects of different glazes, and painted eight plates. First, I sketched a monkey riding on an ox. As Junjun was born in the Year of the Monkey and I was born in the Year of the Ox, I was going to use this plate to tease Junjun, to show her how cheeky she always was to me. As for the other seven, I simply mixed a load of glazes together and then let my feelings guide me as I traced out designs and semi-abstract figures with a piece of bamboo. One of the plates simply had a whirlpool swirled on to it. The vortex of the whirlpool was off-centre, making it look rather unstable. When I put the plates into the kiln I had no idea how they would turn out.

You know, a kiln really is an amazing box of tricks. Porcelain goes into it and is reborn. The heat ranges from a couple of degrees centigrade to over a thousand and the baking goes on from ten or so hours to several days. When you open up the kiln and retrieve the porcelain, you can be greeted with an amazing success or an abysmal failure, a masterpiece or a heap of rubbish! Some make you scream, some make you wild with joy, others make you weep. Each piece of pottery has a fate of its own, impossible to predict. No matter how great the skill that goes in, chance still plays a part. In the past, potters used to burn incense and pray to Buddha on days when the kiln was opened after a firing.

My eight plates were actually brought out on the day of the wedding. Everyone said that the joy of the occasion had been transmitted to the plates. What a shock when the blistering hot mould was broken open! A miracle! This great kiln of yellow earth and red brick had turned out to be the world's greatest art studio. I had put in a seed and it had sprouted into a magnificent work of art!

The plate with the monkey and the ox on it was shiny and bright and looked as though it had been coated in a thick layer of oil. The originally white monkey had been transformed into a golden yellow that was the same colour as Junjun's dress. The paint had spread out in all directions, giving the impression of long hair. The original plan had been for the ox to be dark brown, but when it eventually came out of the kiln it proved to be multicoloured. Because the top half had not oxygenated evenly, several black spots had appeared on top of the white base. The shape and the placing of the spots were so perfect that I wouldn't have been able to paint them better if I'd tried. The background colour had baked into a deep shiny blue that made the monkey and the ox stand out beautifully. The little golden monkey was crowning the ox with flowers that were as pale, soft and delicate in colour as any freshly plucked flower. As a work of art it was beyond my wildest expectations. The other plates were all stunning too, especially the one on which I had swirled the whirlpool pattern. The handful of colours I had used had been transformed into hundreds, and had mixed together in a maelstrom of colour. As you stared at it you felt yourself descending into the bowels of the earth. It was both bold and majestic, but I can't find the words to do it justice. I thought I would go mad with happiness!

Hua Xiayu! Hua Xiayu! I shouted to myself. Haven't you always dreamed of pouring all your creativity into challenging work? Haven't you always believed that you would only break free from the unbreakable shackles of artistic golden rules in a place where artistic success is determined by chance?

Haven't you always believed that only truly innovative creations would be able to defeat those glorious masterpieces of antiquity? Haven't you always said that the strongest fetters on painting are the very tools of painting themselves? Today you've proved every one of those theories!

You've discovered a new world. Look how vast it is!

'The whole world is opening up before us, waiting for us to go out into it and create, not copy.' Picasso's words thundered through my mind. I sat there staring at those plates for half an hour, unable to say a word.

Luo Changgui came over, looked at the plates and was startled into silence. He picked up the one with the whirlpool of colours, then turned round and walked off. When I got married that evening, he had changed into clean clothes and was holding a cloth bag in his hands. He opened the bag and then tore open several layers of tissue paper to reveal the piece of porcelain he was giving me. It was a pure white lotus-leaf pitcher. You could tell at a glance that it was a masterpiece. The edge of each lotus leaf was either curled up or curved downwards; the leaves seemed to flicker and shimmer, as if they were being buffeted by wind. The piece was white throughout. A few veins had been carved with delicate precision into the upper surface of the leaves. The glaze on the pitcher was as fine as jade but when you turned it over you saw that its base was rough and bumpy. There was a contrast between coarseness and refinement, crudity and elegance, motion and serenity, that you wouldn't even find in a museum piece. This was one of the best things that Luo Changgui had ever produced.

He looked me in the eye, as though he were watching to see whether I knew the worth of the gift.

The table was covered with pieces of pottery. It was the tradition here to give pottery at weddings. The highlight of Junjun's dowry was a pair of blue and white vases which had been handed down from generation to generation.

I put Luo Changgui's lotus-leaf pitcher on the table and all the other pieces of pottery seemed to pale into insignificance.

My excitement at the gift evidently moved Luo Changgui. 'Do what you like with it, it's yours!' he said. He was really happy that evening.

The factory workers were really good to me too. They cleared out the inner room for me. Although the walls were crumbling, I completely covered all four with paintings. Landscapes, paintings of flowers and plants, still-life paintings . . . The room contained a whole universe.

Secretary Luo didn't come that day. He said that he had a meeting in the town but I think it might have been an excuse. The saddest thing about the wedding was that Junjun's aunt and uncle didn't come despite several attempts to invite them. Luo Jiaju brought along the second daughter of Cao Jiaxi, the County Party Committee's boss. She was nice-looking and Luo Jiaju looked very pleased with himself. In fact this seemed to make things easier between us and we didn't feel so awkward. However, when Junjun jubilantly produced my coloured plates for everyone to look at, Luo Jiaju's face screwed up with displeasure, as though it had been painted with glue which had now dried. He deliberately avoided looking at the plates and tried to act as though he wasn't bothered; but when the others started teasing Junjun and weren't watching him, he couldn't help staring at the plates. As I was very mindful of how the two of us got on, I kept a careful eye on him. When he arrived he had been carrying a bulging bag which evidently contained a piece of pottery that he wanted to give me. In the end he walked off with it, without taking it out. His face remained tense until he left and he was obviously unhappy.

If other people are jealous of your skill, there's really not much you can do about it.

Luckily, I was so happy that day that no shadow could darken my heart. I had got Junjun and those plates: they were like two boundless canvases on which I could go wild and paint all the beautiful things I felt inside. I believe that I was the happiest person in the world that night.

A driver once told me that driving can be strange. You stop at one red light and then get caught by a whole string of red lights. It's tough luck if you want to speed up. Then you get days when all the lights are green and you can pass unimpeded in any direction. At that moment on the road of life all my lights were green.

The festivities went on late into the night. When the guests had all gone and Junjun was about to lock up, the door handle suddenly moved. The door opened a crack and a black shape came into the room. Junjun cried out in fright and threw herself into my arms. I looked up and saw at once that it was Jet. Had he come to congratulate me on my marriage? I told Junjun not to be afraid, that this was my friend. I told her how I had got to know this dog and then said, 'When I was loneliest, he came to me of his own free will and kept me company. Now I've got you and you're all I need, but I can't drop an old friend, can I?'

This made Junjun laugh. She wrapped her bare arms around my neck and said, 'I only want you. I'm not bothered about anything else.'

'How about that?' I asked Jet. 'Did you hear? That's generous of her, isn't it? This used to be home to the two of us but from now on it'll be home to the three of us. She and I will be in the inner room and you can stay in the outer room. OK?'

Jet seemed a little uneasy when he came into the room. As I spoke he looked at me as though he didn't really understand; but then he came over, sniffed Junjun with his black nose and started wagging his tail happily. He was obviously pleased to go along with what I'd said. I spread out an old piece of felt that I had used for painting in a corner of the outer room. He immediately lay down on it obediently and went to sleep.

From then on, whenever he came he would sleep in the outer room. I carried on treating him the way I always had. On days off, when I was painting and Junjun was doing the housework, Jet would help out by fetching the broom, the fly-swatter, the kettle or the cover for the stove . . . Life was perfect. However,

I still felt an indefinable unease. I'm not sure whether all happy people suffer from this nameless anxiety or whether it was just a premonition of doom.

Chapter 4

The political colour of the little county town had always been a rather insipid shade. Quite a few people didn't even know the names of the leaders of the Party's Central Committee. They just knew that Beijing was 'somewhere south' and their knowledge of the capital did not extend much beyond the design on the eight-cent stamp: Tian An Men and that pillar in front of it with the writhing dragons. When the noise of beating drums suddenly started to resound through the streets in July 1966, people thought that something really important must have happened. When they rushed out and asked, they found out that the Sixteen Conditions* had been proclaimed, though in most cases this did not leave them any the wiser. The people who were beating the drums told them that they must form orderly ranks and march around. A disorganized and noisy rabble therefore paraded around the town. Later that day a meeting was held in the factory and several slogans were pasted up on the walls. The consensus of opinion was that things would settle down again after a few days. What was I doing while all this was going on? I had never taken sides in any of the previous movements. I was only interested in colour, life and beauty; I'd always been a bit of an outsider when it came to these life-and-death struggles. Who could have known that this time it would be so different?

The day of the parade I was standing in front of the firing oven, waiting for a set of new-style painted plates to come out. After the day of my wedding when I had made those eight plates, Luo Changgui had let me take over the plate-painting. One of the young men I was friendly with came over, tapped me quietly on the shoulder and whispered a few words in my ear. I didn't believe him. I thought that he was trying to scare me for a joke; but when I went out into the courtyard to have a look, I saw that a group of people had indeed gathered and that several young men were in the process of sticking up big character posters. When they caught sight of me, they all slunk away. The people there weren't used to taking part in political movements. Even the young men who had been putting up the big character posters quickly hung their heads and left before I could see who they were. The atmosphere felt tense. One of the slogans leapt before my eyes: 'Dig out Hua Xiayu, the rightist who slipped through the net!' I looked at it again, but there was no mistake: it definitely said Hua Xiayu! I felt dazed. How had this started? What did being a rightist or not being a rightist have to do with me? During the anti-rightist campaign I had been like a little pebble way up the beach and the waves hadn't even touched me. I wanted to take a closer look at what had been written on the poster in case I had made a mistake, but I couldn't seem to get my eyes to focus properly. I could see individual characters here and there but I couldn't read line by line. I forced myself to calm down: I wasn't going to learn anything by looking at the poster. I went to look for Luo Jiaju. The previous week the County Committee of the Party had announced that he was to be the factory's 'Head of the Cultural Revolution'. He convened and spoke at all the meetings held in the factory, large or small. Secretary Luo had been put to one side like an old china jar. He was being shunted out of the way.

Luo Jiaju no longer painted vases in the workshop: he had moved to a square office. As there hadn't been time to put up a name plate, a yellow sheet of paper with the words 'Cultural Revolution Office' on it had been pasted up on the door. As soon as I pushed open the door I saw seven or eight people crowded around two or three tables. They seemed to be writing big character posters and leafing through materials. They were obviously startled to see me. One of them immediately moved round to block my line of vision and stop me from seeing what they were up to. Luo Jiaju came up to me and used his board-like chest to push me out of the room, pulling the door to as he went. I asked him what was behind the big character poster in the courtyard and his emotionless voice grated like two pieces of china rubbing together: 'That's your own business. What are you asking me for?'

His face was no longer wreathed in smiles. I noticed for the first time that his pupils were very small. They were an ash-like colour that was somehow much brighter than black would have been. His gaze was like a dagger plunging into my heart.

I was panicking by now. All I could think of was getting back to my room to try and calm down. The route back was festooned on both sides with big character posters. The wet paste hadn't even had time to seep through the posters and the ink on them was still glistening. There was a stink of cheap ink. Every one of the posters had my name on it. I had never been in fear of my own name before. The posters felt like bullets coming at me from all sides.

I suddenly remembered that Luo Jiaju's attitude towards me had seemed a little strange over the last few days. He had been avoiding me. It's true to say that if someone means you harm he will always fear you. He had been keeping his distance from me quite deliberately. Then I also remembered that when we had all been playing chess during the midday break the day before last, some of the young lads had been shouting for us to compete against each other. While we were playing he hadn't spoken to me, but as he moved his pieces he kept repeating the same thing over and over again: 'You asked for it, don't blame me!' Were those words, loaded with double meaning, meant to show that he'd decided to go for the throat? Why hadn't I paid more attention to it at the time? Maybe because when you've got a clear conscience you're not so sensitive to that kind of thing.

As I walked along absorbed in thought, I suddenly bumped into someone. Actually, it was more like bumping into a brick wall. It was Cui Dajiao. He glared at me and shouted: 'I said you were a counter-revolutionary and you pretended you didn't know what I meant. Luo Jiaju never lies. You wait, I'll revolutionize you if it's the last thing I do!' After saying this he delivered a mighty kick to a nearby willow sapling, making it shake from top to bottom. It confirmed my privately-held view that there was a kind of brutality in Cui Dajiao that was always looking for release.

I didn't know where this disaster had come from, nor how things were going to turn out; but I knew that my fate was completely in the hands of others.

That evening, Junjun stood before me, her face as pale as a sheet. Neither of us said a word for what seemed like an age. Time slipped by meaninglessly and then she suddenly asked, 'Why did you lie to me?'

It seemed to be a mixture of reproach and interrogation.

I couldn't stand being questioned like this by the person I loved with all my heart. 'Lie' is such a terrifying word. How could I lie to her? Isn't love about giving yourself unreservedly to the other person?

'I didn't lie to you! I don't know what this is about either. I've never been a rightist. I've always told you the truth . . . You've got to believe me, Junjun!' Every word was loaded with sincerity, just like every brush-stroke when I painted. 'I think someone's out to get me, but I can't think who it is. I'm scared, Junjun!' I could hear my heart pounding. All of a sudden I was overcome by weakness and I burst into tears.

She rested her head against my shoulder and looked up at me with smiling long-lashed eyes. 'No matter what happens to you, I'll stick by you. If they struggle against you, I'll stand by your side; if you

48

get sent to prison, I'll take you food every day; if you get shot and buried . . . I shouldn't say that . . . I'll dig until I find you and then lie down beside you . . .' Her warmth, sincerity and loyalty consoled my aching heart. I felt like someone who, under attack by enemies from every side, suddenly finds a wall against his back. That sturdy wall would protect me. 'I'll sing you a song . . .' She started to hum a tune softly.

I relaxed and my next words were a little lighter. 'I'm not frightened but it's even more important that you don't get frightened . . . you're carrying our baby! We need to be strong for him.'

To tell the truth, I was talking this way to bolster my own confidence.

She smiled at me and nodded as she continued to hum the tune. The sound of the tune drove away my anxiety and worry, comforted me and warmed me. I'd never realized that a song could contain so much . . . As I listened harder and harder I discovered a sort of pain in the heart of the song, a sentimentality and sadness like the faint sound of weeping. Suddenly I felt guilty. How could I ask such a lovely woman to follow me into fear and dread? My imagination began to run riot. I imagined myself being sent far away to the Great Northern Wilderness to be re- formed through hard labour, while she remained all alone in this tiny room. I imagined her sitting under the dim glow of the lamp humming this song and waiting for me to return . . . Or, many years later, setting out with our child and travelling endless muddy roads, crossing snow and ice to find me again. Humming this same tune all the time. I would hear the song from inside my little forest warden's wooden shack and rush out to fold her and our child in my arms. Her long eyelashes would have little pearls of ice stuck to them . . .

The sound of the song faded and my thoughts scattered. She had fallen asleep with her head resting against me. We hadn't put the light on and darkness now filled the room. Moonlight streamed in through the back window, its cold rays brushing her sleeping face. That smooth, lovely face looked so pale, but there was still a smile hovering on the corners of her lips. I suddenly remembered that we hadn't eaten, but I didn't want to wake her up. She was sleeping peacefully, all her weight pressed against my chest so that I could feel our unborn child moving about inside her every now and then. I felt the happiness of an expectant father. The feeling finally made me relax and become drowsy. As I hovered between wakefulness and sleep I was suddenly struck by a whimsical thought: wouldn't it be marvellous if when I woke up it all turned out to have been a bad dream and none of this was happening? In the past I had always wanted to turn dreams into reality; this was the first time I'd ever wanted to turn reality into a dream.

It's not true, it's not true, it's not true . . . All night those few words were jumbled up in a series of fractured but still oppressive dreams. When I woke up the next day, my sense of reality deteriorated further. Not long after Junjun left for work, the back courtyard was filled with big character posters denouncing me and discussing my 'problem' in great detail. It was all to do with remarks I had made expressing dissatisfaction with the 1957 Anti-Rightist Campaign. I was flabbergasted! Every sentence sounded like me, even the tone was correct . . . but I couldn't for the life of me think to whom I had said these things, who could have exposed me. If I really had said those things, how come I hadn't been unmasked as a Rightist long ago? Everything they said was what I had actually felt at the time, but how could anyone know? Had an interrogation machine been developed that could pick thoughts out of one's head?

I wasn't allowed to defend myself. Each of the teams in the workshop put up posters to declare their views on the subject of my 'problem'. I wanted to go back to my room and hide myself away, but when I got there I saw that a large white poster had been papered to the door, warning me that I had to admit my crimes. The name at the bottom of the poster was 'Scarlet Defenders'. I didn't know where these Scarlet Defenders had appeared from. My name looked like the name of a criminal condemned for execution, crossed out with crude vermilion brushstrokes. The situation was utterly hopeless.

That evening Junjun didn't get home until late. I was worried sick but didn't dare go outside. I was scared people would think I was trying to escape. Titanic struggles were taking place outside the factory and the noise all around of people baying for blood and chanting slogans continued non-stop. Once as peaceful as a mountain forest, now it was as though the little county town had been infected with a germ of insanity. Everyone had gone mad. I remembered Junjun saying that the students in her school had already started causing trouble and the longer I waited the more anxious I became. Holding my breath, I listened for the footsteps outside that would announce her return.

In the end she appeared at the door without me having heard her coming. I was shocked by her appearance. Her face was white, even her lips, but her eye sockets were black and her hair was a mess. Someone had cut off her little ponytail! She looked destroyed.

'What . . . what happened to you?'

Instead of replying, she asked, 'Is it true what those posters in the courtyard say? You can't hide the truth from me any longer! The Red Guards* at the school wouldn't let me come home to start with. Then Luo Jiaju came to the school and said that I had been tricked, so they let me go. The Red Guards said that I should persuade you to confess.'

'Confess to what? I admit I had my doubts about the Anti-Rightist Campaign, but I never told anyone! I told you before, I'm not interested in politics. I've never spoken to anyone.'

She immediately fell on the bed, sobbing. 'It's all over, it's all over! You're still lying to me! If you never said anything, how could people know?'

I could only watch her sob until she had cried herself out. I sat there motionless all night long, staring into the corner of the room. I didn't know how I was going to persuade her. I put my hand on her shoulder but she pushed me away. She didn't want me to touch her.

In the morning she left without saying anything.

At nine o'clock everyone in the factory was called to the courtyard at the back. The Cultural Revolution team was there too, but I couldn't see Luo Jiaju. Cui Dajiao had brought some people with him who were all wearing fifteen-centimetre wide red armbands. The armbands had 'Scarlet Defenders' daubed on them in yellow paint. Cui Dajiao dragged me by the collar to the middle of the courtyard. Luo Tieniu was standing next to me; it seemed that he was in trouble too. He stood there all hunched up and with his head hanging down, his battered shoe-box frame looking as though it had been squashed even flatter than usual. The atmosphere was extremely tense. Hardly anyone was talking and the only sound was Cui Dajiao's blustering voice.

Suddenly the courtyard gate opened and two teams of Red Guards marched smartly in, each guard carrying one of those wooden practice rifles used for military training. I could see a woman in their midst. Junjun! The Red Guards made the two of us stand facing each other two metres apart. Then they brought over two dunces' caps made of white card and tied them to our heads. Poor Junjun, it was such a cruel sight! Her deathly white face was the same colour as the hat. I wanted to pull the hat off and throw it away, but no matter how brave you are there's nothing you can do in a situation like that: courage becomes stupidity and everything is turned upside-down and inside out. I felt a rush of blood to my head: 'It's nothing to do with Junjun! It's me and no one else!'

A swarthy, tough-looking Red Guard then asked: 'So, you admit that everything in the posters is true, then?'

'Yes! Yes! Yes!' My only thought was to get Junjun out of this mess.

The Red Guard continued, 'Good, at least you've confessed part of it. Now tell us who you told.'

I wanted to confess but there was nothing to confess, so I said: 'I can't remember.'

'Talk!'

'It's too long ago, I'll have to think. Anyway, I admit it's all true.' I thought that saying this was the only way that I was going to rescue Junjun from her humiliation. I would have confessed to murder for her.

The Red Guard turned round and poked Junjun viciously in the arm with the wooden practice rifle. 'This morning you were still saying this wasn't true, but he's just admitted it all. Do you know it's a crime to shelter counter-revolutionaries?'

'Don't blame her. I lied to her! She didn't know what was really going on!'

Luo Jiaju suddenly appeared to my left and said: 'Repeat what you just said. You hid all your problems from Luo Junjun!'

I could tell from the stricken look in Junjun's sombre eyes that she didn't want to hear anything, but I had no choice. The protective instinct I felt for her replied: 'It's true, I lied to her all along.'

54

I don't know whether saying that protected her or harmed her.

Luo Jiaju looked incredibly pleased with himself but he put on a sarcastic tone of voice. 'Lying to women, eh? What a splendid person you are!' He tried to look furious.

I looked up at Junjun and saw that the face under the hat was livid. The eyes looked as though they had lost all their lashes and they were radiating hatred.

Luo Jiaju went over and removed the hat from her head. He pointed at me and said to Junjun: 'Do you still want to live with this person? If not, you can get your things and go home.'

I watched Junjun march unhesitatingly over to our room and remove her quilt and a few other things. The look she gave me as she left was filled not only with hatred but also with contempt.

The remaining Red Guards and Cui Dajiao's Scarlet Defenders smashed my room to bits and then took all the debris into the courtyard and burnt it. Every now and then the crowd of people all around me would wave their fists and chant slogans. I kept thinking that it was like a scene from a badly written farce and that it actually had nothing to do with me.

From then on I was like a cruelly used toy. On one occasion I was almost killed. Cui Dajiao said that I had been born wrong and he was determined to re-fire me in the clay oven. He tipped a bucket of glaze over my head and pushed me into the oven. He was about to seal the door of the oven with bricks and mud when Luo Changgui, waving a book of quotations and shouting, 'Carry out struggle using words, not swords', pulled me out of the oven. But the worst was the time when they carried my painted plates out from the workshop and into the courtyard. I had poured blood, sweat and tears into those plates and there must have been over five hundred of them, each one of them different. They arranged them into rows of ten and tens of rows, covering almost the entire courtyard. Then they gave me a hammer and ordered me to smash every last one. Those plates were so delicate and exquisite that you had to handle them with the utmost care for fear of damaging them. I don't know whose evil idea it was. It was like taking a mallet to my heart, but I had to smash them. Funnily enough, after I'd smashed the first few I thought about hitting myself over the head and finishing it all; after I'd smashed about fifty I felt as though I wasn't smashing plates at all, just ordinary rocks. I was a machine, smashing another every couple of seconds. I was working in time to the cries of Cui Dajiao and his cronies: 'Smash! Smash! Smash! Smash!' I started to smash with real gusto. My whole body was filled with a mad energy which was trying to explode its way out. My waving arms seemed to change shape and the sound of breaking pottery roared through my veins, but I was hitting too hard and the broken fragments bounced up in my face and made me bleed. I wanted nothing, nothing worried me any longer, and I cared about nothing! But the shouts of the Scarlet Defenders grew weaker and weaker. Some people didn't shout at all and obviously had misgivings about the whole thing. These were people who had been making pottery for many years and who knew that what I was destroying was incredibly precious.

Several days later, the focus of the factory's struggles shifted to Luo Tieniu. As Luo Tieniu had managed to offend a lot of people, they were even rougher with him. The Scarlet Defenders made me kneel down on the broken fragments of pottery each day and read out the posters criticizing me until I could recite them from memory. This went on for two days until my knees were all bloody. The fragments tore my trousers and embedded themselves in my flesh. When I went back to my room in the evenings, I had to dig them out one by one, but I didn't feel any pain. I missed Junjun more and more. I worried that she might still be persecuted. The fact that she resented me and hated me didn't matter. She couldn't really hate me. As long as she remembered our true love, she wouldn't need me to explain anything else and she would come back. As she had said, no matter what happened to me, she would follow. I truly believed it. But why hadn't she come back? The empty space by my side felt as if it was empty for her. Waiting for her was the only reason that I carried on living.

Chapter 5

One morning, before I even had a chance to go outside and kneel before the posters, Cui Dajiao and his gang came rushing into my room. They dragged me into the courtyard, gave me a beating and accused me of having torn down the posters. That was a capital offence then. Luckily I wasn't very tough and I collapsed after a few blows. This made them lose interest. If I had been made of sterner stuff, I would probably have been beaten to death. I looked up and saw that the posters had indeed been torn to shreds. Who could have done it? Obviously someone who wanted to get me killed.

The Scarlet Defenders ordered me to paste up all the scraps which had been torn down so that the rips and tears would no longer be visible. I spent the whole day pasting.

When I was in my room that evening there was no wind outside and everything was very still.

The struggles and beatings, which had raged unchecked for several days, now abated. In the still of the night, the sound of threats and the drone of slogans being shouted only came intermittently and from a distance. Suddenly my heart leapt to my mouth as I heard the sound of paper being torn in the courtyard. I tiptoed over to the window and looked out. There was no sign of anyone in the moonlit courtyard, but I could see a piece of broken china glinting faintly. Then I saw someone squatting in the corner. As the light there was particularly dim, all I could see was a black shadow ripping up the posters. Who was it? Whoever it was clearly meant to ruin me. I shouted out in panic: 'What are you doing?'

The person froze but didn't stand up. He seemed to be crouching in the dark so that I wouldn't see who he was.

'Who is it?'

Suddenly, he ran off as fast as his legs would carry him.

As soon as he ran I recognized him. It wasn't a person at all, it was a dog. Jet! What was he doing tearing up the posters? To retaliate on my behalf? But how could he understand what the characters said? What was going through his head? Later I guessed that he must have been watching what had been going on during the day from some hidden vantage point and must have seen me kneeling in front of the posters as a punishment. He might have thought that the posters were a danger to me and decided to come and tear them up at night. I was certain that was it!

The next day, because the posters had been torn up, I was once again dragged off to be punished by the Scarlet Defenders. They placed a jar on the ground and told me to kneel on it. If the jar fell over and broke I would be accused of 'counter-revolutionary damaging of national property' and be handed over to the Public Security Bureau for 'punishment in accordance with the law'.

Although I only weighed fifty-one kilos I still had to be very careful kneeling on the jar. Very soon, the jar started to wobble and Cui Dajiao's cronies gathered round to yell at me that I had better not knock the jar over. They were terrorizing me just for the hell of it. The more nervous I got, the more the jar wobbled. In no time at all it went over.

Suddenly I heard the sound of barking. It was Jet. He was standing about three metres away and snarling furiously. Each time he snarled he jutted his jaw ferociously. His black fur was bristling as if he were wearing a big overcoat and in his fury he looked extremely dangerous. He'd come to save me!

Two or three of the Scarlet Defenders started attacking him with the wooden practice rifles but he was too bold and agile for them. He jumped back and forth and didn't get hit once; in fact, he even managed to tear one of their trouser legs with his teeth. As none of them dared approach him, he eventually forced them into retreat.

Cui Dajiao came out to see what was going on. These last few days, the cruelty and malice in him had been laid bare for all to see as he did what he pleased. All the muscles in his body were trembling with excitement and he looked more cunning than usual. He told me to get off the jar, then he passed me one of the practice rifles and ordered me to attack Jet.

'If you don't, it means that you're joining him in

persecuting the masses. Then we'll beat you to death!'

I caught the rifle and called to Jet. As soon as I called him, he stopped barking. He hesitated a moment, then walked slowly towards me. Cui Dajiao's Scarlet Defenders retreated a couple of metres. They were all scared of Jet, but they shouted out, 'What are you waiting for? Hit him!'

I raised the rifle, but Jet didn't move an inch. He thought I was playing. He got up and started wagging his tail happily. He jumped about and tried to catch the rifle with his front paws. How could I hit him? I spoke to him in a low voice: 'Go. Go away . . .'

But he wouldn't go. He started rolling around on the ground, trying to get me to play with him.

Cui Dajiao yelled at me: 'If you don't hit him, we'll chop you to bits!'

Then I hissed at Jet: 'If you don't go, I will hit you!'

Jet got up and looked at me. He seemed to understand what I was saying, but still he wouldn't go. He wanted to protect me and he didn't believe I would hit him. His eyes were full of trust.

'I'm going to count to three,' shouted Cui Dajiao. 'If you don't do anything we'll kill you both! I'm counting . . . One, two . . .'

Just as he was about to reach three, I gritted my teeth and struck. I heard a stricken yelp from the other end of the rifle and Jet jumped up in the air almost as high as me and the rifle. When he landed, he spun round towards me as though he was going to attack. The fur on his neck was all on end. He was furious!

The Scarlet Defenders shouted out excitedly: 'Go on, Jet! Bite him!' But he didn't attack. His tail drooped and he stared at me with a look of misery and reproach. Then he turned round and ran off, disappearing round the corner of the warehouse.

To this day I've never forgiven myself for hitting him: the thought of it has haunted me periodically. I don't just hate myself; I despise myself for what I did.

I stared at the empty corner by the warehouse in a kind of daze, but Cui Dajiao's rabble didn't let me stay in a daze for long. They said that I had taught this dog to persecute the masses and then they gave me another vicious beating. This time they paid special attention to my hands. They said that my hands were 'Black Hands'* and they ordered me to take a brick in one hand and use it to smash the other hand. I smashed away until I could no longer hold the brick in either hand.

That night I was at the end of my strength.

My bed had been smashed the day the Scarlet Defenders had raided the house. There was a straw mattress on the floor. My backside had been flogged during the day and I found lying on it painful, so I lay on my stomach. I stretched my two smashed hands out in front of me. They felt as if they were on fire and this way I could let them be soothed by the cool night air which was seeping in from the outside.

The pane of glass in the door had been smashed by the Scarlet Defenders so that they could keep an eye on me. The electric lights and all the electric wiring had been ripped out in case I tried to commit suicide. It was pitch dark. I stared outside at the hazy moonlit courtyard and two words kept turning over and over in my mind: black night, black night, black night . . . I felt the pleasant sensation of my body slipping downwards. I felt as though I was no longer lying on the floor but on a kind of downy sea. Then I felt a small hand that was soft and warm stroking my own injured hands. It felt so beautiful and real . . . not like a dream at all. It must be Junjun. No one else would come to care for me and comfort me at this hour. Only her.

But when I opened my eyes and looked, it was Jet! He was licking my injured hands with his soft tongue. He hadn't borne a grudge against me for hitting him, but had come looking for me.

'Jet!' I called out his name painfully in a low voice.

He was sitting on his haunches in front of me. Behind him, a patch of door was filled with moon-light, resplendent and hazy at the same time. In contrast, the bulk of his body seemed to absorb light and was as black as pitch. I couldn't even see his eyes. The moon's rays outlined him with a silvery, dazzling, furry aura. He looked like a mighty lion. No, to be more accurate, he looked like a god, dignified, sublime, benevolent. At the same time he seemed to embody the spirit of fanatical loyalty.

'Jet . . .'

I was deeply moved. My voice started to tremble and break.

He stood up and walked over to my side. He lay down close to me and didn't make a sound, except for a sort of affectionate growling noise which came from his stomach. When his paw had touched my skin a moment ago, it was still cool with the night breeze; now the warmth of his body kept me warm.

I shut my eyes and enjoyed the feeling: the warmest, purest and rarest feeling in the world.

Afterwards, he came to see me at irregular intervals. He always came at night to comfort me. He would disappear again before daybreak.

Later, after a criticism and struggle meeting,* it was decided that I should be sent to Qing Shi Shan to be reformed through hard labour. The Scarlet Defenders escorted me on to the back of an old truck. Cui Dajiao was the driver. Luo Jiaju was sitting in the cab too. He was going because a great criticism and struggle meeting was being prepared in my honour at Qing Shi Shan. He was to be one of the Masters of Ceremony.

I saw Luo Jiaju only rarely. Although I was like a mouse or a bird in his claws, he never openly took part in the Scarlet Defenders' operations against me. He spent all his time dealing with Luo Tieniu. I thought it was probably because both of us were artists and the question of face would have made it embarrassing for him to deal with me harshly himself. I was so stupid! It was he who had come up with all the worst ideas, he who had brought the Red Guards to attack me and Junjun, he who had forced me to smash all those plates, he who had got Cui

Dajiao to destroy my hands. He just never showed his face, that was all.

Seven or eight of the Scarlet Defenders were sitting around me in the back of the truck. My arms were trussed up in case I tried to jump out. The truck drove out through the factory gates to the sound of a hundred or more people shouting slogans. As the truck went through the county town, people in the streets stared into the back and pointed at me. As we passed the town gates, one of the Scarlet Defenders suddenly shouted, 'Look! We're being chased!'

Being chased? By whom? I craned my neck to look out. It was Jet! Where had he come from? How did he know that I was being taken away?

He was running frantically and soon caught up with the truck.

There was no glass in the rear window of the cab. I could see the back of Luo Jiaju and Cui Dajiao. I could also see past them to the road ahead through the windscreen. Luo Jiaju turned round and asked who was chasing. The Scarlet Defender said, 'It's that black dog!' Luo Jiaju whispered something into Cui Dajiao's ear and the truck suddenly started to pick up speed. They seemed to be trying to lose Jet. In the gaps between the Scarlet Defenders' shoulders I could see Jet chasing desperately. As the truck jolted along, I would spot him one minute, then lose sight of him the next. He was getting smaller and smaller. Finally the truck stirred up a cloud of dust and everything was obscured. Although I couldn't see him there was the faint sound of barking in the distance. They only slowed down again once they had lost Jet.

Some time approaching midday, the truck stopped at a small canteen by the side of the road. They took the rope which was binding me and tied it to a wooden beam in the back of the truck. Then they all got out for their lunch. About twenty minutes later I suddenly saw a little black shape appear on the road in the distance. It gradually increased in size and when it got to about a hundred metres away from the truck I recognized it as Jet. He tiptoed over. By the time he was standing in front of the truck I noticed that his colour had changed: he was covered all over in a layer of dust. I shifted myself to the side of the truck and he tried several times to throw himself into the back; but try as he might, he couldn't scramble up. He must have been exhausted by his marathon. I couldn't help him as my hands were tied. In the end I stretched a leg out of the truck and he grabbed hold of my foot. With a mighty heave, I managed to get him aboard. He buried his head in my chest and barked a couple of times. The noise that came out sounded like a piece of wood being scratched, probably because his throat was so dry. I couldn't understand what he was saying but knew why he was saying it. Nothing in this world will ever move me more than that did. I wept and my tears landed on the dense fur covering his cheeks. They glistened there and made it look as if he was crying too.

Just then, Luo Jiaju and Cui Dajiao emerged from the canteen, their faces flushed and bellies swollen with food and drink. As soon as they got in the truck they saw Jet and shouted: 'How did that animal catch up? It must be a demon!' Jet didn't wait for them to grab him. He jumped on to the roof of the cab, baring his teeth like he was going to fight them, but he was knocked to the ground with a swipe of a wooden practice rifle.

He got up again and barked at the truck from the side of the road. 'Quick! Start it up!' said Luo Jiaju.

Cui Dajiao started the engine and was about to move off when he saw Jet in front of the truck about eight or so metres away. He was lying in the middle of the road. He was determined to stop the truck even if it meant dying in the process. His air of fatalism, dignity and calm seemed to stun the madmen in the truck. They seemed overwhelmed by a mystical force and not one of them shouted. Cui Dajiao pressed the horn a few times but Jet remained there, motionless. He showed no fear in the face of the rumbling truck. Luo Jiaju turned to Cui Dajiao. 'Run him over!'

Terrified, I begged Jet to move: 'Get out of the way, Jet!'

I don't have any children, but that's exactly how I would have shouted if one of my children had been in mortal danger.

Jet lay there watching the truck that would run him over with a calm that a human being would have found hard to match.

The truck seemed to be stationary. There was a strange atmosphere.

Luo Jiaju shouted at Cui Dajiao, 'What are you waiting for, I told you to drive over him!'

After a pause which lasted a couple of seconds, Cui Dajiao shouted back, 'All right! Let's go!'

The truck started up. It raced towards Jet in a rush of wind. Piercing through my cry of despair and the violent swerving of the truck, I heard Jet yelp from under its wheels. My heart wrenched violently, and in the stabs of agony which followed I felt my whole body become as formless as a puff of smoke. Everything before me ceased to exist. I ceased to exist. In the split second before I lost consciousness I felt I should be grabbing hold of something; but I couldn't hold on to anything. The world turned into a pure, absolute white and I thought, 'This is what it feels like to be dead . . .' I'll always remember that feeling until the day I die.

Chapter 6

Qing Shi Shan is a huge quarry. The work there was physically exhausting. You collected slabs of rock from one side of the mountain, then pushed them back across the mountain in a wheelbarrow to get to the workshop where they were ground into powder for making china clay. The loaded wheelbarrow was extremely heavy and the only way to get it moving and to stop it from slipping back when you were going up a slope was to bend your body so that it was almost parallel with the handles. The locals, who had lived and worked with the rocks for years, did not altogether resemble the rocks in terms of angularity of feature or roughness or hardness; but their taciturn natures did make them seem peculiarly rocklike. Just after I had arrived, the working party I had been assigned to called me over. Each member of the group was carrying a rock, ready to hit me, so it seemed, if I said the slightest thing wrong. The leader of the group was called Qin Laowu. The skin on his face was drawn as tight as a drum. There wasn't an ounce of fat on his body and every muscle looked as if it was carved out of rock. They asked me whose money-box or wife I had stolen. In the past, all criminals sent there for punishment had to undergo this. Mountain people hate thieves and adulterers, and telling the truth earns such criminals a good beating. I told them that I was an artist and that apart from my 'thought problems' I hadn't done anything wrong. They threw the stones they were holding on to the ground and were kind to me after that. But they warned me: 'Don't try to escape.'

As I said, Qin Laowu was the leader of this little band. He was very assertive and no one could beat him in an argument. When it rained or snowed and the mountain paths became difficult, everyone had to strain together to push the barrows across the mountain. He would take the lead and make up work songs about the other workers' wives off the top of his head. The others used to curse him until they were blue in the face, but at the same time they gritted their teeth and responded. No one was allowed to slack. The only wife that Qin Laowu didn't talk about was mine. I didn't know whether that was because I was an outsider and he felt awkward about making fun of me, or whether it was because he knew that I was worrying about Junjun constantly. Our little baby had been in her womb for six months now. I saw the baby so clearly in my dreams; he was just like Junjun. Junjun had once said that a couple's baby always looked like the one who loved the other more.

One day when the wind was howling outside, Qin Laowu came into my room carrying a jug of rice wine. 'Come on, son,' he said, 'let's have a drink. When we're drunk there's something I have to tell you.'

I asked him what it was but he wouldn't say.

When we were about half drunk, he finally said, 'Your wife wants to divorce you.'

'Get lost!' The drink had gone to my head and I felt like lashing out. 'I ought to kill you ... aren't you scared?'

His red eyes looked like a pair of hawthorn berries. He glared at me and answered: 'Scared of you? Your wife aborted your child ... your son!'

My face flushed and the alcohol rushed to my head. I grabbed the wine jug and smashed it to smithereens against the wall. Then I bunched my fists and, as if I were beating a drum, I pummelled Qin Laowu's rock-like chest. 'Give me back my son,' I wept, 'give me my son.' Qin Laowu didn't move. He stuck out his chest and let me hit him. When I had no strength left he suddenly gave me such a blow that I was knocked across the length of the bed. The punch was like a cannon blast and I suddenly found myself sober again. 'What kind of man are you?' I heard him say, 'You're gutless!' His eyes were popping from his head.

In all my life, I've never been dealt such a sweet blow. It seemed to smash the heavy stone which had been pressing on my heart.

I climbed into bed and cried.

He saw me crying but did nothing to stop me. When he saw that I had more or less cried myself out, he pulled out a turnip from his pocket and snapped it in two: 'Eat it!' He threw me half and continued, 'Cool down and you'll be fine.' He drew back the door curtain and walked out.

It's strange. Something as tragic as that should

have driven anyone mad; but I was able to stand it because of him. My eyes were full of tears and my mouth was chewing cold turnip; but inside I felt OK.

My wife and my family were finished. I didn't worry about Luo Junjun any more. Is there anything more heartless and chilling than a woman doing away with her own flesh and blood? My poor son! I had decided on a name for him but I can't bear to say it out loud now. Although he was never born, it's like hearing the name of a dead relative . . .

At this moment, a lovable furry shadow floated slowly upwards from the depths of my heart. Jet!

The shadow stayed with me and kept appearing, even when I wasn't thinking of him. It wasn't a kind of sick hallucination; it was a beautiful vision. When I was pushing the barrow, I imagined him using his front paws to push the barrow's wheels; when I clambered up the bank after washing in the river, I imagined him bringing me my shoes; at mealtimes, if there was bone with a scrap of meat on it, I imagined myself saying, 'Lift up your left paw, Jet!' Cleverly, he would immediately raise his left paw. Then I would say: 'Lift up your right paw!' He would lift up his right paw and then I would put the bone into his bright pink, slobbering mouth . . .

But if the scene where I had hit him with the wooden practice rifle ever came before my eyes and I saw that mournful, resentful and injured look, I would immediately avert my gaze and stare hard at something else, trying to re-bury the resurrected memory. If ever I heard Jet's piercing yelp when he was crushed to death under the truck, I would desperately hum a couple of bars of a Chairman Mao song, trying to smother an agony that was buried too deep in my heart for me to escape from it. I wanted to forget the past completely. Forget the porcelain factory, forget the painted plates, forget Luo Jiaju, Cui Dajiao and Luo Junjun . . . forget Jet's past and forget that he was dead. I wanted him to carry on living in my affections, accompanying me. I truly believed that as long as he could stay with me, I could put up with any hardship.

Haven't you found that the very thing you most want to forget is the one thing you'll always remember?

I couldn't spend all my time wallowing in my imagination, so I made myself a little dog out of clay, about seven centimetres long. I painted it with some black ink. It looked just like Jet, especially its expression. To start with, I put it on my bedroom windowsill. That night, the moon's rays shone into the room and coated his outline with a silvery sheen, just like the night after I had been beaten and he had sat down in front of me and licked my hands. He had brought me so much comfort and warmth. But the sight brought back unbearable memories and I rushed over to the windowsill and took it away. I left the window as bare as the world around it, its latticework quietly lit by the heartless moonlight. At that moment my heart was ashes. The only feeling I had left was my hatred for Cui Dajiao.

Little did I know that through the clay model of Jet I would meet Cui Dajiao once again.

Chapter 7

The following spring one of the local children came running into my room. He thought the little black dog sitting on my table would be a nice toy and demanded that I give it to him. He couldn't know the special place occupied in my heart by that little black dog. When he saw that I wasn't going to give it to him, he ran out and fetched a clay dog to swap with mine. I cried out in surprise when I saw the clay dog and the child stepped backwards in fright. The dog was so lifelike, it was as though it had just bitten me.

I can honestly say that I had never seen such a brilliant clay toy before, such a dazzling and audacious work of art! It was so bold! The artist who had created it made other daring artists pale in comparison. The clay dog's head was about half the size of its body and its legs were frankly like four knobbly sticks. Its tail looked like a sweet potato and was stuck up cheekily. Its eyes stared at you and its mouth hung open foolishly; it looked like a grasshopper about to jump on your nose. It had a garland of flowers around its neck and for some unknown reason it had a large pearl on top of its head. Joyous, vigorous and strong; as soon as you saw it you could see that it was an expression of the love of life felt by

Chinese peasants for thousands of years. Its plain white coat had been daubed with brush strokes of red, yellow, green, blue and black. The primary colours hadn't been mixed or blended; each colour was clearly defined and separate. The brush-strokes had a straightforwardness and precision unmatched even by the Old Masters of Chinese art. You could never learn how to do that in the Academy. The professors at the Academy relied on their training when they painted; peasant artists relied on their instincts. Which one was real art? If you tried to copy it, each of your brush-strokes would be sure to look as lifeless as each stroke of the original was full of life. Isn't it odd? Who would have believed that true art could flourish in the soil of a poor backwater together with the peanuts and sweet potatoes? Particularly in an area fond of a blue so dark that it sapped the life from any other colour near it.

I asked the child where he had got the clay dog. He said that the 'smelly old man' had sold it to him. I asked around and finally discovered that the 'smelly old man' was from Tai Tou village in the neighbouring county. Apparently they could all make clay figures in that village.

When I had a day off work, I stuffed all my money – four dollars and seventeen cents – into my pocket, grabbed a gunny sack for carrying the clay figures, and slipped out of Qing Shi Shan in the morning mist without telling anyone. After all, my reform was supposed to be taking place under prison conditions; if I had told anyone, they wouldn't have dared let me go.

When I got to Tai Tou village, I asked a peasant if he knew where I could find the 'smelly old man'. As soon as the peasant heard what I was buying, he took me to a woodshed at the back of his house. He removed several bundles of firewood to reveal a room full of clay figures. The largest were about half a metre and the smallest about the size of a fingernail. Clay men and clay horses, clay cats and clay dogs, all decked out in red, green, blue and yellow. Each one had its own individual character and each one stared at you with its own particular expression. The room swam before my eyes and I had to make myself calm down before choosing a few of the best examples.

Thinking that I was some sort of dealer in odds and ends, the peasant started to bargain over the price. I was worried that I wouldn't be able to take the figures if he asked too much, but to my surprise he only asked for two dollars. Two dollars for these treasures? I excitedly gave him three dollars. He happily helped me pack the figures up with rice straw and he also gave me some old cotton wool to pack the bottom of the gunny sack. As we were chatting he told me about someone called 'Magic Scissors Huang' who lived in Ban Pu Zi village on the other side of the river. Old Woman Huang was a brilliant paper-cutter who originally came from Chang Dao in Shandong Province. When she had come to the village her dowry had included one hundred and eight clay figure casts; casts of the hundred and eight generals in *Outlaws of the Marsh*. Someone who had seen them said that every one of them looked better than the actors who took their roles in the play. Old Woman Huang had never been able to bring herself to use them and make clay reproductions. They had apparently been handed down through generations of her family; even in Chang Dao, hers was the only set.

When I heard this, I ran almost all the way there, carrying the clay figures on my back. As I crossed the river, my footsteps felt really light and the patches of foam I stirred up were like fields of crystal flowers.

When I got to the village and found Old Woman Huang, she said that I had found the wrong person. However, when she heard that I was an artist, she wept and told me that one hot summer's day in 1966 she had been forced to hand over the casts for her hundred and eight generals to a work team sent by the Commune. They had denounced them as symbols of the 'Four Olds' and had smashed them to pieces. I thought of my painted plates and suddenly felt very close to her. She fished something out from a trunk. It looked like a clay bowl but was in fact a fragment of one of the casts, the only piece she had managed to retrieve. Half a face was carved on it and you could see at a glance that it was Shi Qian!* The crafty expression shone out from the impressions in the bowl-like surface. I rubbed my hands together with delight at finding this masterpiece. It looked as if it had just come out of the kiln and I didn't dare touch it for fear of burning my hands. I could well believe that there had only been one such set in the world. Now even that was gone.

Old Woman Huang seemed touched by my enthusiasm.

Her face was covered in fine, long wrinkles. When she was worried, her face looked as if it was covered in cobwebs; but now the lines suddenly grew shallower and her face seemed to burst through the cobwebs as she laughed. She climbed over her young granddaughter who was sleeping on the *kang** and lifted up the *kang* mat. She pulled out a cloth bag and a sheet of folded black paper.

She fished out a pair of shiny scissors from the cloth bag and unfolded the sheet of paper. The sheet was about the same size as the surface of a table. 'I'll do you a papercut,' she said, and the scissors started flashing as they moved in her hand. As an accompaniment to the crisp sound of the scissors cutting through the paper, a flurry of fine black confetti fell to the floor. She would fold the paper one way, make a few cuts, then fold it the other and make a few more. The paper was like a little swallow beating its wings. Roughly half an hour later, she spread out the metre-square sheet of paper on the bed and laughed: 'It's been two years since I did any papercuts, so I'm a bit rusty. Anyway, this is called "Goldfish Pond"!'

I blinked, unable to believe the miracle before my eyes. Can you believe that a pair of scissors and a sheet of paper is all it takes to recreate the gaudy splendour of the sea bed, in all its mystery and its matchless beauty? The twists and turns in the cuts flowed as freely as the imagination, as fine as hair one moment and as thick as an oxtail the next;

78

crooked cuts and large expanses of black, all bursting with life . . .

I had always had a fuzzy kind of half-formed theory about ancient Chinese art. I believed that the magnificent capriciousness, the awesome majesty, the boldness and the creativity, the beautiful self-indulgence of Han and Tang art had eventually ended up mirroring the gradual and steady decline of the feudal dynasties, slipping inexorably into blandness and vulgarity. But this was only true of palace art; the dynamic mainstream had survived unbroken to the present day . . . in folk art! From the ancient cave paintings, the potteries, the bronzeware, the stone reliefs, the terracotta warriors . . . right up to the New Year folk pictures, the clay toys, the papercuts, the wax prints and the porcelain of today. An irresistible artistic spirit still flowed throughout our vast nation. Why didn't our Fine Art Academies move out amongst the people? I looked at this ordinary-looking old villager and thought excitedly that this was where all our Picassos and our Matisses were. This was a queen of modern art!

She told me that she had grown up by the sea and was therefore familiar with all the different kinds of fish depicted in the papercut. She pointed them out to me: seahorses, cuttle fish, flounders, silvery pomfrets, wolf's fang eels . . . but she never included sharks in her papercuts. A shark had taken a bite out of her husband's belly when he was diving for pearls at the age of thirty, and had made her a widow. She said that in Chang Dao this style of black papercut used to be stuck on ceilings. People used to look at them as they lay on their *kang* at night, staring at them until they fell asleep. She didn't want to see a shark every day; she would never get to sleep.

I nodded in understanding.

I didn't know how to repay her. All I could do was give her everything I had left. I fished out the rest of the money in my pocket, but this enraged her. She frowned again, and all her wrinkles stood out in straight lines. She said that it was probably the last time that she would ever do a papercut and the last one ever was not for sale.

I folded the papercut into four, then stuck it between two tatty old mats before putting it into my gunny sack. As I said farewell to this Old Master, I waited until she wasn't looking, then surreptitiously slipped the remaining one dollar and seventeen cents under the pillow of her granddaughter who was still fast asleep.

On the way back, it started to rain. It bucketed down and I got soaked to the skin, but I didn't care. My only worry was that the damp might ruin the treasures I was carrying in the sack. I took refuge in a roadside café. The café consisted of one large room with reed and mud walls and a thatched roof. In the centre of the room was a stove which had been converted from an old petrol drum. There was no chimney, and the heat and the smoke coming from a pot of noodles boiling on the stove created a kind of fog. A group of drivers and travellers was huddled around the stove. Some were lying on straw mats, fast asleep, using their torn old cotton padded overcoats as quilts; those without overcoats pressed together for warmth. Maybe the room was too hot or maybe it was just a reflection of the stove's flames, but all their faces looked as red as tomatoes. I told the manager that I didn't have any money and asked whether it would be OK if I rested a while and had something to eat. Seeing the sorry state I was in, the manager gave me a big bowl full of the noodle soup. It was more soup than noodles but I was grateful to get anything to eat at all. I had been walking all day, I was drenched right through and my stomach felt like a wide-open bag waiting to be stuffed with food. I took the bowl and went at it like a pig at a trough. I gobbled the whole lot down in one go, even devouring the grit at the bottom of the bowl.

I couldn't delay any longer. If I went back any later, Qin Laowu and the others would think that I had run off. I rejoined the road, but when I had walked just half a *li*, a big truck drove up from behind. I quickly walked to the side of the road to get out of its way, but it slowed down and stopped beside me. The door opened and the driver called out, 'Get in!'

Delighted to have come across such a good-hearted person, I called my thanks to the driver and clambered up into the cab, putting my gunny sack down by my feet.

The truck started up again and the driver asked me, 'Where are you going?'

His voice was very familiar. I turned round to look at him. He drew hard on his cigarette and as it glowed I saw that it was Cui Dajiao! This was the truck which had crushed Jet to death!

'Stop the truck and let me out!' I demanded.

He ignored me and drove straight on.

'Let me out!'

'Stay where you are. I'll drive you back!' he replied. The truck was moving really fast.

I jumped up, intending to grab the handbrake. 'I'm not riding in your truck,' I shouted. 'I'll never ride in your truck!' I tried to snatch control of the steering wheel from him.

Braking suddenly, he brought the vehicle to a halt. After he had composed himself, he said, 'All right then, get out!'

I got out of the truck and he drove off with a squeal of tyres. I hurried back as fast as I could along the dark and muddy road, but my shoes kept coming off in the mud. It took me over five hours to get back to Qing Shi Shan. I removed the various items from my gunny sack and put them in a place at the bottom of a cliff where the rain couldn't reach them. Having stowed them away safely, I covered them with grass. When I got back to my house, I could see that the oil lamp was burning inside and that Qin Laowu was sitting there grim-faced with a few of the others. I was sure that Cui Dajiao must have reported me, but it turned out that Cui Dajiao must have driven straight on.

'We've been good to you. What were you trying to do?' one of the men shouted at me angrily.

'I didn't run off!' As the rain was coming down outside with renewed force, I was forced to shout.

'Where did you get to?' the same man asked.

I told them the truth. Qin Laowu looked at me,

puzzled. He told me to take him to see the clay figures, obviously disbelieving my story. They all put on their raincoats and Qin Laowu brought his large torch which took four batteries. In the driving rain I led them to the foot of the cliff and opened up the bag. Qin Laowu shone his torch into the bag and then looked up. From the expression on his face he was obviously wondering why on earth I had bought those things, but when he spoke it was to say, 'Take those things back inside quickly!' He threw his raincoat over to me and I told him gratefully, 'I'd never run off.'

'I'm not worried about you running off. I thought you'd committed suicide!' He ducked under one of the other's raincoats.

I carried the raincoat instead of wearing it and enjoyed the feeling of letting the icy rain run down my neck. I won't die, I thought happily to myself, not while the world still has so many wonderful things to offer.

Chapter 8

Over seven hundred days of forced labour went by.

It was announced that I was 'a person with a difficult past whose problems have been resolved'. I could 'return to the porcelain factory without stigma and work under observation'. Of course there was a contradiction between the two proclamations. Don't laugh, that's just about the level you can expect from a place like that! It was actually a very generous resolution, and one that I fought for long and hard.

Starting from when I discovered the Shi Qian clay figures and papercuts, I spent two years scouring the whole mountain region. I got to know some stonemasons who had been carving Buddhas in the Northern Wei tradition for generations. They had stopped carving during the Cultural Revolution and now earned their living breaking up rocks. Although the majority of them could not read or write, their artistic sense was highly developed. They were also extremely loyal. If you appreciated their art they would be utterly devoted to you. They took me up into a ravine once and dug up statues of Buddha that they had secretly buried. The statues were as good as anything by Michelangelo, Rodin or Henry Moore. They wanted to give them to me, but there was no way that I could carry them. As I had nowhere to store them either, we ended up burying them again.

Inspired by these masters of folk art, I achieved a very important breakthrough in my own understanding of art. My head was filled with new ideas and I yearned to put them into practice. I had to get away from Qing Shi Shan as soon as possible and return to the porcelain factory. I had the means to create the most original painted plates of the era.

So I started to work like a demon. During the day I would go up the mountain to gather rocks, and in the evening I would push the huge millstone, turn the mill's big iron drum and grind the rocks into china powder. Every day I worked until my bones ached. They all told me to stop but I wouldn't listen and they said I was mad.

The day I left, Qin Laowu gave me a certificate to present on my return to the factory. This certificate was very different from the registration note given to me by the Academy long ago. The registration note had been black but this was transparent. My heart had become transparent too; you could see it through my breast.

Qin Laowu told me, 'I'll see you off!' and carried my bag for me.

I felt a little sad to be leaving. Since that day when I had bought the clay figures he had let me go wherever I pleased on public holidays. He didn't know what I wanted to do on these trips; he just saw that I was happy and let it go at that.

He accompanied me right down to the mountain pass, a journey of over twenty *li*. He didn't utter a word during the whole journey, but his throat kept making a sort of stuttering noise as though he had something stuck there. Did he really find it so difficult to express his feelings? As we reached the crest of a hill, he returned my bag to me and said, 'Well, son, this is as far as I go! As we agreed, you go your way and I'll turn round and go my way. No turning back!' His words overwhelmed me. I wanted to hug him, but the rock-like calmness of his demeanour made me control myself.

I nodded my agreement.

We turned away from each other at the same moment and went our separate ways. I walked straight to the bottom of the hill, forcing myself not to look back; but when I got to the point where the path wound round the corner and marked the end of the mountains, I couldn't help looking back. To my surprise, Qin Laowu was still where I had left him and had not moved a step. He looked like a mountain goat, standing motionless on the hill. For a moment, my whole body was suffused with a rush of emotion and I shouted out, 'Qin . . . Lao . . . Wu, Qin . . . Lao . . . Wu . . .'

But he couldn't hear me; he was too high up.

I waved my arms at him energetically, but he just turned round and walked off. I started crying but didn't wipe away the tears. I walked along, letting the tears stream down my face, unsure whether the tears were acting as a release or whether I was simply enjoying them. I only wiped my face once I had stopped crying and my cheeks felt tight.

Once again I stood outside the factory gates with my luggage, looking in. But this was very different from the first time. If you want to analyse the feeling, it was a mixture of sour, sweet, bitter and hot. When I got to the back courtyard I told myself that there was no way that Junjun would still be living there. And of course she wasn't. The door to the little room was boarded up with criss-crossing planks, just like that big character poster with my name struck out by a big cross.

When I got to the office I found out that Luo Jiaju had long since been transferred to the County Committee to act as deputy chairman of the Revolutionary Committee. A young newcomer was in charge of implementing policy. He was perfectly well aware of who I was. His gaze swept over me, then he picked up a tool to prise open the door to my room. Everything inside was covered in a thick layer of grey dust. A moment later, the young man handed me a bundle of odds and ends, saying, 'Luo Junjun took all her things away. She said that these were yours. We have a list of the items which Luo Junjun took away. You can check it if you like.'

I shook my head and laughed bitterly. Why bring back painful memories?

I opened the bundle and had a look: materials, a palette, a brush, a few paint-spattered and tatty old clothes, a single glove, a torn pillowcase . . . a whole load of things which I had forgotten about until I saw them again. Then to my surprise I saw a plate! I wiped the dust off with my hands and my heart beat with a clang like a copper gong. It was the 'Monkey Riding an Ox' plate that I had fired on our wedding day! The mischievous little golden monkey was sitting on the back of the multicoloured ox and crowning it with flowers. Pleased with the trick it had played on the ox, the monkey was waving its arms in the air and was in danger of falling off the ox's back. The plate and the picture on it made me feel the warmth of old times like a warm wind sweeping away all the cold and bitterness. I was suddenly desperate to call up before my eyes the images of yesterday and the day before that and the day before that. Then I suddenly wondered why Junjun hadn't taken the plate with her when she had come to collect her things. This plate was a symbol of our togetherness. The significance of it hit me and I felt as though a desolate, gritty wind was blowing through my heart.

Through Luo Junjun's aunt, I was able to meet Junjun again. I told her: 'I didn't cheat you. That day when the Red Guards were holding the criticism and struggle meeting, the only reason I said that I'd cheated you was that I didn't want you getting hurt. I still don't know to this day how or why I'd been accused . . . You must have been heartbroken when you thought that I'd cheated you.'

To my surprise, she wasn't in the least bit interested in this important point. She replied coldly, 'I don't care about all that. There's no point!'

'No point? What do you mean?'

'No point at all.'

'I don't understand what you mean.'

'I have to be practical!' she replied.

This last sentence revealed how she was thinking nowadays. I suddenly felt that there was no feeling in

88

her long-lashed eyes; the eyes were like two puddles of dead water and the lashes were like stalks of withered grass. Her outline was no longer hazy, but sharp and well-defined.

Maybe you're wondering what happened to all her artistic sensibilities and poetic feeling. Well, life is the greatest sculptor of all. Not only can it alter a person's external appearance, it can also alter a person's heart, which is something that no other sculptor can achieve. Once a person becomes practical, there's no turning back. The two of us were like oil and water now. I had originally planned to try my hardest, but when I saw her stomach, flattened again since she had rid herself of our child, then I . . . I went to file the papers for divorce.

I picked up the divorce certificate the same day. I took it together with the 'Monkey Riding an Ox' plate and went to the wasteland outside the back window of my room. I dug a hole in the ground using a willow branch, placed the divorce certificate on top of the plate and then buried them both. Then, in accordance with what Luo Junjun had once said, I picked a great armful of yellow chrysanthemum heads and laid them on the earth. I have never been so calm, so collected and so tranquil as I was at that moment. A strange thought crossed my mind at that point: what if, hundreds or even thousands of years later, an archaeologist were to unearth that beautiful plate? The divorce certificate which I had placed on top of it would have long since rotted away, and no amount of research would reveal the story behind the plate . . .

I felt slightly at a loss.

That evening I went to see Luo Changgui. I had heard that he had been paralysed for quite a while now and wasn't expected to live much longer. I always remembered him pulling me out of the oven.

Luo Changgui was in extremely poor shape. The noise of his wheezing was louder than the sound of his voice. His eyes were cloudy and the flesh on his face had simply collapsed; the bones stuck out in ridges and looked like the river plain behind my room at low tide. I felt as though he was going to slowly melt away on the bed before my eyes and that his round, clumsy, dear body would never sit up again.

When he saw me, his nostrils flared with excitement and he said something that he had never been willing to say before: 'I . . . I really admire your craftsmanship! If there are people like you, chinaware will never die out. If only your name was Luo . . .'

I suddenly remembered something that I had been carrying around inside me for a long time: 'Master, how is it that everything you make is so alive? I mean your bottles and jars . . . even your little dishes?'

Luo Changgui listened and his long-paralysed body suddenly moved slightly, as though he wanted to sit up. My words had obviously touched a key buried deep down and his body was momentarily electrified. He told me to pick up the gourd-shaped bottle from the table and take a close look at it. As I turned it over in my hands he asked me what I could see. I replied: 'It's got your fingerprints all over it.'

His eyes flashed with happiness: 'Vitality is in the hands. Remember that! When you're making pottery, the last thing you want to do is to make it completely smooth. Those prints are the pottery's "eyes". You're an artist. Without your eyes you'd be dead. You live through your eyes.'

I suddenly recalled those ancient ceramic figurines, cooking stands and urns, twisted and crude but full of character; I thought of Old Woman Huang's scissor cuts, rough and ready but self-assured and confident. Surely that was the whole secret of art. I was desperate to find the key to unlock this secret. I was convinced that Old Luo could give it to me.

'Is there anything else I should know about these "eyes"?'

Luo Changgui mumbled to himself a moment, as if undecided. The light gradually receded in his dull eyes and he said, 'I'll tell you next time.' He called over the girl who was caring for him – I don't know whether it was his daughter or some more distant relative – and he asked her to bring over two objects. One of these was a writing brush sticking out of a worn-down old copper lid; the other was an old red box. 'This brush,' he started, 'is excellent. I've used it for thirty years, but I won't need it again, so you take it. Open the box . . .' As he waited for me to open it he breathed raspingly.

The box was for holding Mah-jong* tiles. It was as fine as jade but on closer inspection proved to be made of porcelain. The flowers decorating its surface had been carved and looked vivid and real. It was a masterpiece of the porcelain-worker's art. Luo

Changgui told me, 'Look after it well. Don't let anyone smash it on the pretext that it's one of the Four Olds. You understand quality, so you take it! I haven't got anything else to give away . . .'

I was speechless with gratitude.

Later I mentioned Cui Dajiao and Luo Changgui said: 'That was retribution. It was a wide mountain road, there was no ice and he'd been driving for more than twenty years . . . but he ended up crashing into a ravine. Lucky he was single and didn't orphan or widow anyone. But he wasn't like Jiaju, he was just stupid . . . he never used to be so vicious. What made everyone go like that in those days?'

'I'll never forgive him for killing Jet!' I replied.

'What? You mean that dog? You're doing him an injustice . . . he never killed your dog. He told me himself.'

'He lied to you. I was in the truck at the time.'

'No, no, no . . . He told me. He tried to swerve out of the way but he was too close and he couldn't swerve far enough. He clipped one of the dog's hind legs.'

'Really?' I shouted out loud. I still couldn't believe that Cui Dajiao had spared Jet; he would never have done that! But then I remembered that just as the truck was rushing towards Jet it had suddenly swerved violently. 'Is it true? Then Jet's still alive?' I didn't dare believe it. I didn't want to raise my hopes only to have them dashed.

'Yes, he's still alive, honestly. I saw him myself. After you left he came back to your room and barked for days. One of his hind legs was lame . . .'

Suddenly Old Luo's room was filled with light. Who should I thank? Life is so wonderful! It never lets you despair. It always makes things turn out for the best. It always makes it up to you in the end. It gives you a tomorrow and a day after tomorrow and a whole wide future. When you're stumbling around in the darkness it opens out a road at your feet . . .

I started searching high and low for Jet. I asked everyone I met, but I got different answers; some said they had seen him and others said they hadn't. Finally I got a definite clue. A travelling cigarette-seller told me that he had seen a scrawny dog sitting down by the side of a country road about twenty *li* to the west of the county town. He had looked as though he was weak from starvation and the cigarette-seller had taken pity on him and given him a scrap of bun. The dog had eaten it and had followed the cigarette-seller a while before disappearing. The cigarette-seller said that one of the dog's legs had seemed a little lame. After hearing this news, I was filled with hope.

On my days off I would buy a piece of meat, tie it up with string and carry it around with me. I searched throughout the county town, and ranged far and wide in the surrounding countryside. I searched the fields, the roads, the towns and villages, all the time looking for Jet, looking, looking. I began to realize that the world was too vast and that if you lose something in it it's not that easy to find it again.

It was just another Sunday. I was carrying the lump of meat and I had been walking non-stop from daybreak until noon, still not finding the slightest trace of Jet. In the end I was so exhausted that will-power alone was forcing me to search, not emotion. But I never abandoned the hope of finding him again; I believed that in the beginning he must have searched for me like this too. As I reached the outskirts of a village, I was finding it hard to force my legs forward and I was losing my sense of bal-ance. I bought a bowl of rice gruel from a little stand by the side of the road and rested a moment with my legs stretched out in front of me. All of a sudden I heard shouts: 'Hit him! Hit him! Hit the dog!' I looked over and saw a gang of little yobs whip-ping a dog with a willow branch. The dog wasn't moving, wasn't trying to defend itself. It was lying by the wall, as though it was dead. It was a black dog!

My Jet? My heart beat faster for a moment and I rushed over.

My first glance told me it was Jet; when I looked again I wasn't so sure. Although the dog was indeed black, its fur didn't seem as long as Jet's had been and its body had been worn down to a shadow. It was covered in dust and extremely dirty. It didn't seem to have the energy to stand up to the attacks of the children; it just lay there on its side with its eyes closed.

'Jet!' I tried calling it.

It jumped up at the sound and the children re-treated a couple of steps in fright. Its stick-like and hairless legs trembled as they supported its weak body and it leaned forward. It lifted its gaunt head and stared at me with huge eyes.

'Lift up your right paw, Jet!' I told it, my voice breaking.

With a great effort it shakingly gave me its muddy right paw. Jet! My Jet! It was my Jet! I stretched out my arms and pulled him to me fiercely. I hugged him tight and felt his body trembling so violently that I thought I was trembling too. In fact, I was shaking. I could feel him burrowing his head enthusiastically and excitedly into my chest. I felt like I was once again holding the whole world in my arms . . .

'Needless to say, I'll make sure I never lose him again. I take him everywhere I go. I always have to travel soft sleeper class because of him; it's safer, they don't check so much. He's really smart. If you tell him not to make any noise, he won't make any noise. I'm scared that if I part from him that'll be it, I'll never see him again . . . These last few years he seems to have got old. He doesn't go out wandering any more and he hardly eats anything. That beautiful fur of his will never grow back either. He stays beside me all day, but if he ever hears the sound of a car starting up he looks really nervous. His eyes bulge, he growls and the hair on the back of his neck stands on end. Anyway, that's the end of the story. Now you know what's in the cardboard box!'

After this 'unknown' artist, Hua Xiayu, had finished telling me his remarkable life story, my throat choked with sympathy. I looked up at the cardboard box. I couldn't hear the slightest sound coming from it, but I was certain that hidden inside was a tragic tale and a loyal and restless spirit. Hearing about Hua Xiayu's past, I worried about his present: 'Are you still painting plates?'

Laughing, Hua Xiayu shook his head. His laugh seemed to be directed at himself. I asked him why. 'If I tell you, you'll be sure to laugh at me! When I was sent back to the factory, I started off in the warehouse painting plates. That changed after a couple of weeks, though. It was such a small thing . . . One day I was walking along one of the roads on the outskirts of town. It had been raining and the scenery looked as though it had just been scooped out of the water; it was vivid and fresh and bright. Then a patch of white appeared up ahead, a white so pure that it seemed suddenly to make all the other colours jump up an octave. It made my heart light up in happiness and excitement too. As the patch of white came closer, I saw that it was a white-shirted Luo Jiaju. I hadn't seen him for two or three years. I don't know, maybe I was affected by the beautiful rain-washed scenery or his pure white shirt . . . The fact of the matter is that when I saw him I immediately forgot what had happened in the past. He asked me how I was in a concerned tone of voice. I told him that I was painting plates and that I had loads of new ideas which I hoped would help me turn out quality work. The next day, without a word of explanation, I was sent to work at the factory's kiln instead, firing the porcelain. Wasn't I stupid?'

'Not at all, just a little naïve, perhaps.'

'Yes, you're absolutely right. That's what I am. But anyway, I really don't think I lost out. Working

96

at the kiln I've been able to achieve a better understanding of the laws of firing. The kiln workers all
reckon that thirty per cent of the art of making
porcelain is in the actual moulding; the other seventy
per cent is in the firing. They also say that if you
don't understand firing, you don't understand porcelain. It means that I now have a better idea of how
the plates are likely to turn out. It's strange, but all
the people who have harmed me have ended up
helping me too. Why do you suppose that is?'

I was startled by his words. The ideas in my head
refused to take shape and I couldn't say anything.
This strange person was making my thoughts career
out of control, and I couldn't answer him. Instead, I
asked him: 'Did you ever manage to get Luo Changgui to explain the significance of those "eyes"?'

'No. He died the evening of the day I saw him. He
didn't tell me because he'd decided to take his secret
with him to the grave . . .' Hua Xiayu sighed. 'He
would give away family heirlooms to a stranger, but
not his craft. Conservation dictates that in the beginning, every step we take is along a path previously
trodden by our predecessors; but in the end this
allows us to develop a style of our own and our art
carries with it a greater sense of inaccessibility and
mystery. But Old Luo was very generous to me, you
know. Even those few words he said to me allowed
me to progress to a deeper level. If I ever get a chance
to go back to the workshop and paint again in the
future . . . I'm very confident, do you know that?'
His eyes shone like stars at dawn.

The train carried on through the dark night and

across the frozen countryside. Most of the other passengers were asleep and there was no one in the corridor. The only noise was the loud but rhythmic sound of the heavy train rattling across the joins on each section of track. You could almost forget where you were.

'Are you tired?' Hua Xiayu looked at the grubby watch on his wrist, with its cracked glass: 'Oh, it's half-past five. It'll be getting light soon. We'll be there in about an hour. I'm really sorry, I've kept you up all night.'

'No, no, no. The story's not finished yet. You said that all your troubles came because of what happened in 1957. You still haven't said who made up that stuff about you.'

'No one did.'

'So did Luo Jiaju make it all up?'

'No, he was just using old material. He got that stuff from a dossier.'

'If no one made anything up about you, what was in the dossier? I don't understand.'

Hua Xiayu hesitated a moment, then he told me the truth.

'OK, OK . . . About a month ago I came up to the north-east on this same train. When I got to Shenyang railway station I heard someone call my name. It was a woman called Yang Meimei . . . I didn't tell you her name when I mentioned her before. It was that girl I'd been going out with when I was at the Academy. Anyway, she's married now. As soon as I saw her face and clothes I knew that she had done OK for herself . . . No prizes for guessing where she's working! She was out on business and had never dreamt that she might bump into me. She hadn't seen me for many years and I guessed from her startled expression that she thought I had changed a lot. We had only been chatting a minute or so before she dragged me to a quiet place and asked me whether or not I had run into trouble during the Cultural Revolution. She then proceeded to tell me in an earnest and penitent voice that during one of our rendezvous at the Temple of Heaven, I had expressed my doubts and dissatisfactions with the Anti-Rightist Campaign. When she'd heard this she'd been frightened that my terrible ideas might impede my progress. Full of innocence and sincerity, she had reported every word to the local Party branch. As a result, everything I'd said went into a dossier. During the Cultural Revolution, the porcelain factory searched her out so that she could verify the contents of the document. She had guessed that this must mean that I was in trouble. Although she was worried and felt guilty, she didn't dare write to me and ask. Now she said, "My stupidity must have cost you dear!" Chilled from the inside out, I felt as if I had swallowed a bucket of icy water. I laughed bitterly. She really had cost me dear! At the same time I felt a kind of retrospective terror: after she had informed against me, why had she carried on acting as though she loved me? If I had stayed on at the school, in all probability I would have married her. How could she have lived with me with a clear conscience? It was unimaginable, spinechilling!'

'You should have told her that thanks to her you

lost a wife and child and were almost killed. If she's really got a conscience, you should use it to make her life a misery!' I retorted angrily.

'Everyone has a conscience, but some people listen to it and others ignore it. The fact that she was prepared to tell me the truth must mean that she listens to hers.'

'What did you say to her?'

'I told her that I hadn't been beaten up and that everything had been fine. I told her that her question surprised me.'

'But . . . did she believe you?'

'Of course not. But she didn't ask me any more questions. She preferred to believe that it was the truth. You're a writer. You should be able to understand that. What I told her let her carry on living happily and with an easy conscience. When we parted she pressed a load of stuff into my hands — sweets, cakes, sausages — I couldn't refuse. She was in such a state that she even gave me one of her woollen gloves. I helped her escape from herself. She looked as happy as a little bird flying out of its cage, and her voice even chirped like a little bird. What? Are you laughing at my stupidity? You think I was over-generous? No, I may have had to do several years' hard labour because of all that, but why should I dump it all on another soul? She isn't a bad person; let her be happy!'

I was very moved. I gazed with affection at this warm but unlucky person. Carried away, I said, 'Forget the past. The future's bound to be better than the present.' Because of my own despair with life, the words came out flat. They sounded loud and empty, but they're the kind of thing that people say.

His reply surprised me. 'No. If I died today, I would still thank life for everything it has given me. If I carry on living, it'll be time for me to start repaying life.'

As I listened, I felt as though I was slipping unconsciously into a world that was at once enchanting and moving, but also threatening. I, a person who had always been terrified of life, who had always been apathetic to it and tried to keep a safe distance from it, suddenly felt its hot waves surging and pounding against me . . . I was silent. When you feel a flood of emotion like that, it's better to keep it inside you and let it eddy around slowly. That's the best feeling of all.

The windows of the train started to lighten. The things outside the window began to take on their colours. Could the fact that I suddenly started noticing colours be due to the influence of this artist's perceptions?

Hua Xiayu stood up and put the various items by his side into a bag. Then he said, 'I have to get off the train . . . this is where we part. I hope everything goes well for you!'

'Thank you . . . And I wish you . . .' I thought a moment and then I said, 'I hope I'll see your painted plates soon!'

His eyes shone. It was obviously the thing he wanted to hear above all else. 'You certainly will,' he said, 'you certainly will!' It sounded as though he was reciting an article of faith.

The train started to slow down.

After getting down the cardboard box, he bent over and put his mouth to the little hole in the corner: 'Did you sleep OK?' He spoke as though to a child. Then he said: 'We're home. Don't make any noise!'

I leaned over. 'Is it OK if I have a look?' I was anxious to see this remarkable dog.

An instant later, the train stopped. The hazy shadows of the station, the station building, the platform and the railings all appeared in the window out of the wintry fog. I had a quick look inside the box, but it was as black as pitch and I couldn't see anything. I could, however, smell that unique aroma of animal fur.

'Um, can you give me a hand? I have to get through that ticket barrier safely. I can't fiddle about with things over there, I might get found out. No, no, there's no need for you to get out too, that's fine.' He carried the portfolio case at an angle on his back and hoisted the cardboard box on to his left shoulder. Carrying his battered old case with his right hand, he said, 'Can you get my ticket out for me? It's in the pocket of my overcoat . . . Thanks. Stick it in my mouth, will you, I'll hold it with my teeth. That's it, that's it. Uh . . .' He couldn't say anything to me with the ticket in his mouth, so he smiled his thanks to me.

When he got off the train I didn't say anything else. I gave him a look of farewell which also conveyed my good wishes and a little sadness at parting. From the window, I watched him join the loose crowd of people. When he got to the ticket barrier, I felt a moment of anxiety for him. I saw the ticket inspector take the ticket from his mouth and ask him something. He shook his head, probably saying that he didn't want the ticket for claiming expenses, then he went through safely. From the other side of the railings, he turned round, craned his neck and looked in my direction. I waved to him, but as I had switched off the light in the carriage he probably didn't see me. He turned and walked away . . .

As I watched him walking slowly away, still holding the cardboard box, my heart was overwhelmed with a kind of melancholy. What should I have wished for him? What would his future be? And yet . . . These last few years I have met lots of others like him as I travel around the country. They've experienced all the hardships the world can throw at them, but on the surface you can't see the slightest trace of their suffering. Sometimes it's hard to believe it when they describe the rough and bumpy roads they have travelled! They're just like miraculous magic bags. Life stuffs them full of the roughest, the toughest, the spikiest things imaginable, and no matter how tough it gets, they never burst at the seams. In the end, everything gets quietly digested. Their hearts and their eyes still view life positively. Even someone who despairs of life utterly will not lightly leave it. Isn't that because of life's enchanting richness, its mystery, its deeply hidden hopes? No matter how weighed down we are with woe, we Chinese always soldier on . . .

As I wandered aimlessly in the current of my own

thoughts, I gradually became aware of a piercing light. The train had left the station and it was already daybreak. Outside the window a turbulent icy river twinkled under the rays of the winter sun.

Glossary

Big character posters One of the 'Four Bigs' – speaking out freely, airing views fully, holding great debates and writing big character posters. These posters were used to denounce wrongs and were one of the armoury of weapons used against counter-revolutionaries.

Black Hands An expression used to describe anyone suspected of counter-revolutionary activities.

Criticism and struggle meeting Meetings at which a person's 'crimes' were denounced (criticism) and at which that person would be physically abused (struggle).

The Four Olds Old Ideas, old culture, old customs and old conventions – the targets of a political campaign in late spring 1966.

Jin The Chinese measurement of weight: approximately 500 grams.

Jingdezhen A town in Jiangxi province famous for its porcelain.

Kang Chinese heatable brick bed.

Li The Chinese measurement of distance: approximately 500 metres.

Mah-jong A Chinese game for four, played with 136 or 144 pieces called 'tiles'.

Red Guards   Members of a militant youth organization in China in the 1960's.

Shi Qian   The 107th general in order of appearance in the novel *Outlaws of the Marsh*.

The Sixteen Conditions   Decision of the Central Committee of the Chinese Communist Party concerning the Great Proletarian Cultural Revolution. The decision, consisting of sixteen points, outlined the scope of the Cultural Revolution. The points included boldly arousing the masses, not being afraid of disorder, and the correct handling of contradictions among the people.

Soft sleeper class   Chinese trains generally offer four different classes of carriage: soft sleeper, hard sleeper, soft seat and hard seat. Soft sleeper is the most luxurious (and therefore the most expensive) and hard seat is the least.